MONEY BAY

An Original Screenplay

By

Freeman Emerson

Forward offers by FAX to: 904-829-5773
Or email to proud@aug.com

Represented by
S&S Keshner Agency
P.O. Box 4522
St. Augustine, FL 32085-4522

COVER ART

By

STARR EMERSON

MONEY BAY

CAST

ANNIE - A young woman: "I always get what I want, but it's never what I expect."

MITCH - A man: "Young girls are like puppies; they're cute. Sometimes they pee on the rug, but they're cute."

JIMBO - A young man: "Big fish eat little fish, and sometimes little fish are poison."

VICTORIA - An older woman: "A woman like me is always with somebody."

CARL - Victoria's rich husband: "We baited the trap with something he liked, and when he came sniffing around, I shot him."

SYNOPSIS

A young woman becomes involved with two men on a boat that she charters for a dive trip in paradise.

They sail into crime, conflict, love and murder. A classic movie with a strong supporting cast and story.

- Sexual tension and a clash of egos, erupts into violence.

- Wealth and power, versus survival of the fittest.

- The last man standing isn't always a man.

FADE IN

EXT DAY OCEAN UNDERWATER

The light of the sun is fragmented on the surface as seen
from below. It is dispersed by a splash as JIMBO enters the
water. He wears a mask, snorkle, fins and a brief bathing
suit. He swims down, down, down deep to the bottom. He is
lean and tan. His long hair flows behind him. His movements
are methodical. When he reaches the reef on the ocean floor,
he slowly searches for his objective. He looks under a
coral shelf. A green moray eel looks back at him. He ignores
it. He continues his search. A shadow glides by over him. He
looks up to see a shark moving away. He is unafraid. He
looks down and sees the antennae of a lobster sticking out
beneath the coral shelf. Jimbo holds himself motionless on
the ledge in front of the antennae. He shoves his hand
quickly under the ledge. The water is clouded by swirling
sand and rising bubbles. From out of the confusion, Jimbo
kicks smoothly to the surface.

EXT DAY OCEAN

Jimbo surfaces shooting up out of the water. FREEZE FRAME
Jimbo has a broad smile on his face as the glistening water
runs off of him and he triumphantly holds a giant eight
pound lobster over his head.

MATCH DISSOLVE

INT DAY   APARTMENT

FREEZE FRAME PHOTO Jimbo with lobster.

As the CAMERA PULLS BACK from the FREEZE FRAME PHOTO of

Jimbo with the big lobster, we see ANNIE sitting at a desk in

her apartment. Her hair is pulled back away from her face

and she wears .reading glasses. There is a distant look on

her face and a slight smile as she stares at the photo. She

wears a white blouse and a suit skirt with the jacket thrown

over the back of her chair. On the desk in front of her is a

computer surrounded by manuscripts and correspondence

methodically arranged. Next to the desk is a window with a

protective metal grid. The room contains a loft bed and a

kitchenette. There furnishings are sparse but there are

adequate electronics: television, vcr, stereo, kitchen

appliances etc.... There are posters on the wall of a very

handsome young man, NEAL, advertising deodorant spray. At

the rear of the apartment is an exterior door held closed by

a safety chain. Neal is at the door. Leaving the door ajar,

he comes over behind Annie and bends to kiss her on the back

of her neck. At the same time he reaches into the pocket of

her suit coat and takes out her wallet. He returns to the

door and she continues to be preoccupied with the photo. At

the door he puts money through the opening and a white bag

is slipped back through to him.

                              NEAL

                    Keep the change.

Neal turns from the door after closing it and securing an

additional lock. He goes to the counter of the kitchenette

and takes out two separate white cartons and opens them.

                               NEAL

        I ordered Chinese.

                               ANNIE

           Oh, I hope you got lobster for me.

Neal comes over to her as she places the photo on

the desk and turns in her swivel chair. He ceremoniously

gives her an open carton and a pair of chopsticks.

                               NEAL

           Don't I know you? Lobster!

As he returns to eat at the counter, she uses the chopsticks

to take something solid from the thick white sauce in the carton.

                          ANNIE (disappointed)

           Why is it that I always get what I want,

           but it is never what I expect?

They both eat; she at the desk, he at the counter. Annie

looks at the photo on her desk.

CUT TO

EXT DAY QUAY

The quay is at one side of a tropical harbor. A few boats

are tied up at the seawall and NATIVES are unloading them.

From an old wooden motorsailer, a man throws down a large

canvas bag stenciled "Air Mail." Women carry mangoes in

baskets which they take to the stores that stand in a row

across from the wharf. In the middle of the row is a bar

with a big sign, "Non-Select" across the front which is open

to the harbor.

INT DAY BAR

The bar is horseshoe shaped, one side toward the quay, the
other toward the inside entrance opening on to the street.
At the bar facing the harbor, Jimbo sits with a beer in
front of him. There is a dive bag on the floor and a
speargun leans against the counter. On the seat to his right
is a cloth backpack.He picks up the backpack and places it
in front of him. From inside he takes an address book and a
stack of the Freeze Frame photos. A man, MITCH, enters from
the street and takes the seat where the backpack was. He
wears long pants and a tee shirt. On his head is a blue
watchcap with a silver dive helmet insignia pinned to it. He
has a black and white cat, PUS N' BOOTS, under one arm and
sets him on the floor at his feet as he sits down. A girl,
DEE, who works behind the bar, without instructions,
automatically gets a tall lime water for the man and a dish
of milk for the cat. Mitch looks over in front of Jimbo at
the photos.

                              MITCH
              Nice bug. A bit small, but nice.
                              JIMBO
              Thanks. I'm Jimbo.(notices watchcap
              insignia) Are you a diver?
                              MITCH
              Yeah, names Mitch. Remember that
              hurricane two years ago when they needed
              somebody to clear the channel in St. Agnes?
                              JIMBO (impressed)
              I'm a diver too.

                         MITCH

          You need money ?

                         JIMBO

          I have a job on the Firefly if I can dig

          up some charter business. I'm here to

          see the dog.

Mitch takes the dish of milk from the counter and puts it on
floor for the cat.

                         MITCH (to cat)

          Hear that, Pus? He wants to see the

          diving dog. (to Jimbo) Pus isn't

          impressed.We can use good crew.

                         JIMBO

          No thanks, Pus. I'm an instructor. I'll

          send a few more of these pictures to

          my ex-students.

INT DAY APARTMENT

Annie is standing by the open window dressed as before in
suit and heels. Neal is in the loft bed watching television
The TV PICTURE is a close up of Neal.

                         ANNIE

          You've been watching that tape for two

          years. Wouldn't you like a change of

          scenary?

                         NEAL (excited)

          Yes. I'd like to go out to Hollywood. I

          know I could get work. I...

                          ANNIE (flatly)

We can't afford it.

Annie moves away from the window. She changes from her work

clothes into a sweat suit as they talk.

                          NEAL

Let's not pay the rent.

                          ANNIE (upset)

And stick my stepfather with the bill

again. We're lucky that he let us move

in here for the rent control price after

they got married. He could have sublet

and made some real money.

                          NEAL

Maybe you could borrow from your credit

union?

Annie goes over to her desk and looks for something.

                          ANNIE

I always wanted my own place in the city

and a good job in publishing.Shit!

Neal jumps down from loft and goes over to the open window.

                          NEAL (bitter)

You're a victim. That's your problem.

You reek of it. The second you open this

window, every thief in town can smell

it.

Annie finds her keys under a manuscript. Neal slams the

window shut. Annie rushes to the window and Neal jumps out

of her way.

> ANNIE (angry)

Don't worry about thieves. My step-dad

has insurance.

Annie throws the window open and heads for the door. Neal

gets out of her way. She begins opening the latches.

> NEAL (polite)

You really don't want me to go away

and leave you alone. That's it. You're

co-dependent.I saw a teevee show.

Annie opens the door and looks at a poster of Neal on the

wall.

> ANNIE

I always wanted a good looking boyfriend

like the ones in the magazine ads.

You're the answer to my prayers.

> NEAL

Wait. Don't go now. Let's talk this out.

Annie goes out and leaves Neal with his mouth open.

> ANNIE (yells OFF CAMERA)

Maybe I should have prayed for a man.

INT BAR DAY

Mitch and Jimbo sit at the bar. Jimbo is playing with a

coin, moving it magically between his fingers. Dee is behind

the bar watching him.

> MITCH

Relax. He'll be here soon. Everybody on

the quay will stop to watch.

                            JIMBO

                    Does he really dive?

                            DEE

                    Him dives, mon.

From the street entrance, VICTORIA comes into the bar behind

them. She is chic and secure. She wears a sun dress, heels

and gold.   She checks out the bar. Dee motions with her

head and Jimbo and Mitch turn to check her out. Victoria

takes the seat next to Mitch. Mitch winks at Jimbo and Dee.

                            JIMBO (under his breath)

                    Go get her, champ.

                            MITCH (to Victoria)

                    I'm Mitch. This is Jimbo and Dee. The

                    specialty of the house is the Penis

                    Colossal ...uh.⌐.miss...

                            VICTORIA (straight)

                    Victoria. Is that anything like a Pina

                    Colada ?

                            MITCH

                    It's bigger and more satisfying.

Jimbo laughs and spits out his drink. Dee shakes her head.

                            VICTORIA (to Dee)

                    There's always a couple like this in

                    every bar in the islands. I'll have

                    the specialty of the house.

She looks directly at Mitch and they both start to laugh.

Jimbo slides a copy of the photo across to her in front of

Mitch.

                        JIMBO

        I'm a diver. I give lessons.

Victoria looks at the photo and hands it back to Jimbo

leaning in front of Mitch. Her gold chain falls against

Mitch's arm.

                        VICTORIA

        I rarely go in the water.

                        MITCH

        If you fell in the water with all that

        gold on, you'd sink right to the bottom.

                        VICTORIA

        I'm sure that if I fell into the water,

        that you would jump in and save me.

                        JIMBO (to Mitch)

        I think she's too much woman for you.

                        MITCH

        Well there's two of us, and I said I can

        always use good crew.

They both laugh. Mitch puts out his hand palm up and there

is the SOUND of a loud smack as Jimbo slaps it.

INT DAY GYM

The SOUND of a loud smack is heard as Annie hits the canvas.

She is in a large room with canvas covered mats on the

floor. There are FIVE WOMEN and an INSTRUCTOR in the room

with her. The instructor is standing over Annie while the

other women watch.

                            INSTRUCTOR (to class)

            Even though I have her on the ground,

            she still has a weapon.

                            ANNIE

            My superior intelligence or my disarming

            good looks.

The women laugh with her.

                            INSTRUCTOR

            Look at those beautiful long red nails.

            (leans down to take her hand) Stick one

            of those in my eye. Come on, Annie.

                            ANNIE

            No. I don't want to hurt you.

The instructor helps Annie to her feet.

                            INSTRUCTOR

            The difference between being a victim or

            a victor is visciousness. You have to be

            willing to hurt someone.

The instructor demonstrates on Annie.

                            ANNIE

            Why is it always me?

                            INSTRUCTOR

            You have to be willing to stick your

            finger in someones eye. Or break their

            nose with the heel of your hand. They

            will bleed. They will feel pain.

                              ANNIE

        But won't that make them mad?

Everyone laughs but the instructor who waits quietly.

                           INSTRUCTOR

        They're mad when they attack you.

        They're angry when you defend yourself.

        They're helpless if you do it right.

        They can't see. They can't breath right.

        And if they want to come after you,

        there is always the knee. Kick it from

        the outside in. As many a football

        player will tell you, it doesn't bend

        that way and it breaks real easy.

                              ANNIE

        I don't think I could ever do any of

        those things.

                           INSTRUCTOR

        Then scream as loud as you can and run

        like hell.But if you can't run...

The instructor's arm shoots out, its finger toward Annie's
eyes.

INT DAY BAR

Mitch's arm shoots out, its finger pointing toward the quay.

Victoria, Jimbo and Dee look to the harbor.

                              MITCH

        Thar she blows. The blue boat with the

        black man and the black dog.

POV MITCH

EXT DAY HARBOR

A small blue fishing boat turns slowly into the wind between

the other boats in the anchorage. As it comes to a stop, a

BLACK MAN goes forward on the deck, picks up an anchor from

the bow and tosses it overboard. A BLACK DOG comes forward

and stands at his side as the boat falls back in line with

the other anchored boats.

INT DAY BAR

Mitch sits at the bar. Victoria is standing next to him. Dee

has stopped her work and is watching the boat. Jimbo gets up

from his seat and heads for the quay.

                         JIMBO

          I got to see this. Mitch, watch my gear.

                         MITCH

          You got it.

                         VICTORIA (to Mitch)

          What happens next?

                         MITCH

          After he ties off the anchor rode, the

          man will dive down to make sure she's

          hooked good and not just hung up on

          a piece of harbor trash. The dog will

          follow to check on the man.

                         VICTORIA

          (looks at Mitch) A woman could use a dog

          like that.

EXT DAY QUAY

Jimbo comes out of the bar and hurries down to dockside.

All of the natives have stopped their work. Everyone's

attention is turned toward the harbor. Jimbo works his way

as close to the water as possible for the best vantage

point.

EXT DAY HARBOR

The black man on the blue boat ties off the anchor rode. The

dog is at his side. The man looks to the quay and waves.

Then he dives off the bow into the water. The dog waits a

second and then jumps into the water after the man. In the

water, first the head of the man disappears and then the

head of the dog disappears beneath the surface.

EXT DAY QUAY

Everyone is watching the water. Jimbo is holding his breath.

INT DAY BAR

Victoria and Dee look silently out at the water. Mitch leans

down and picks the cat up from the floor and puts him on the

bar to watch.

EXT DAY QUAY

Jimbo is holding his breath and counting to himself. No one

else has moved.

EXT DAY HARBOR

First the black head of the man pops up above the surface

and then the dog pops up next to him. The man embraces the

dog and then waves to the people on the quay.

EXT DAY QUAY

Everyone applauds and then goes back to their work. Jimbo

applauds longer and louder than anyone else.

INT DAY BAR

Mitch plays with the cat. Dee brings Victoria her drink.

> VICTORIA
>
> Thank you. It's hard to believe. A
>
> diving dog. But, then it's a Lab. They
>
> like the water.

> MITCH
>
> That's nothing. My cat dives too.

> VICTORIA
>
> Oh, come now. I've had many cats.
>
> They hate getting wet.

Victoria goes to pet the cat and he swipes at her with his

claws.

> MITCH
>
> He doesn't trust you. He wants to know
>
> what a girl like you is doing in a nice
>
> place like this.

> VICTORIA
>
> Everybody has to be somewhere. We have a
>
> cabana and a boat at the casino. But
>
> we're here on business. We have a large
>
> company that I run.

                    MITCH

You say "we." Does that mean that you're

with somebody.

                  VICTORIA

A girl like me is always with somebody.

Jimbo comes in from the quay and sits down. The cat walks

over to Victoria and she strokes him.

                    JIMBO

Did you see that? A diving dog!

                    MITCH

It's easier to keep a cat on a boat.

                  VICTORIA

What's his name?

                    MITCH

Pussy. No matter how bad I get, I always

have Pussy on my boat. But if he ever

gets fleas, its over the side.

Jimbo is playing with the coin again with Dee watching it appear

and disappear in his fingers. Victoria gets up to go, giving

the cat to Mitch.

                  VICTORIA

Don't be cruel. You're lucky to have a

cat.I have to go take care of business.

It was grand.

Victoria smiles at all of them and then exits by the street entrance.

                  JIMBO (to Mitch)

I'll bet you get slapped a lot.

                        MITCH

        I get laid a lot too.

Jimbo opens both hands to Dee and the coin has vanished.

                        MITCH (cont.)

        Jimbo, we have a lot in common.

        We're both divers. (looks after

        Victoria) And we both make things

        disappear.

INT NIGHT APARTMENT

The window is open wide with the protective grid open.

There is nothing on Annie's desk. There are no electronics

left in the room. Annie stands by the door with a look of

confusion and pain on her face. Neal is next to her with

a uniformed POLICEMAN who has a clipboard in hands.

                        NEAL

        She left the window open when she left and

        I had to go out on an audition. I'm

        an actor.

                        POLICEMAN

        I'm a writer.

The Policeman takes out a pencil and begins to write on his
pad.

                        ANNIE

        They got my step-dad's computer with all

        of my work in it.That was my life,

        my career.

                              NEAL

There was my television, my vcr, my video

camera.I use it in my work. My film

camera. My stereo. My CD player.

                            POLICEMAN

Slow down. I can't write that fast.

                             ANNIE

(looking at Neal) This is wrong.

                            POLICEMAN

It happens all the time, lady. Just

be glad you weren't home. That's when

it really gets messy. You're lucky.

Neal takes Annie by the arm pretending to calm her. She is

emotionless.

                              NEAL

Maybe this is blessing in disguise.

                            POLICEMAN

Let's start at the top. First, victim's

name.

                              NEAL

That's you, Annie. You're the victim.

Annie pulls viciously away from Neal and goes to her desk

                             ANNIE

(to herself) Victim or victor?

                              NEAL

Annie, what about the bracelet your

step-dad gave you, and was that fur coat

real?

                         POLICEMAN

          You had a lot in this little place.I

          hope someone had insurance.

Annie straightens herself and turns to them resolutely.

                          ANNIE

          Of course my fur was real. And I had a

          camera and a watch and a ....

DISSOLVE TO

EXT DAY BOAT

Mitch is sitting in the cockpit of a large blue and white

boat The boat is a trimaran with nets strung between the

main hull and the two outer hulls.There is a dodger and

canopy over the cockpit to protect against foul

weather.There is a small rowing dinghy tied off the stern.

Mitch is sitting in the cockpit looking at his watch. He

taps it with his finger. He taps it again. He takes off the

watch and tosses it over the side.

                         JIMBO (OFF CAMERA)

          Hey, mon. Don't be polluting these

          waters.

Mitch looks over the side. He goes to the stern and reaches

down and helps Jimbo to come aboard. He wears a bathing suit,

mask and holds his fins in his other hand.

                          MITCH

          Whoppnen, mon?

                          JIMBO

          Good news, bad news.

                         MITCH

Give me the bad news first. I always

like a happy ending.

                         JIMBO

I got kicked off of the Firefly.

                         MITCH (wary)

What'd you do wrong?

                         JIMBO

Nothing serious. You know that young

girl Dee from the Non-Select.

                         MITCH

Yeah, she's a cute one.

                         JIMBO

Well I was giving her lessons on the

boat and the Captain got jealous and

drunk and started to come on to her.

It got ugly. I stepped in on her behalf

and decked him. Turns out she was coming

on to him behind my back all along.

                         MITCH

Young girls. They're like puppies.

They're cute. Sometimes they pee on the

rug, but they're cute.

                         JIMBO

Well, then, here's the good news. I got

an answer to one of my pictures. She

wants a charter and I got no boat.

                        MITCH

She? Another puppy?

                        JIMBO

I"m not sure. I sent out so many

pictures.

                        MITCH

Do you remember what you told her?

                        JIMBO

Oh, yeah. That I missed them..., that

I missed her very much and thought about

her every day since we'd been apart.

                        MITCH

No. About the charter.

                        JIMBO

One hundred dollars a day plus food.

                     MITCH (thoughtful)

I might be able to help you out.

                        JIMBO

Diving business been a little slow

lately?

Jimbo waves his hand in the air and gives Mitch back his

disgarded watch.

                        MITCH

Slow! It's been standing still. I know

where I can get another one. Meet me on

the quay tonight after dark.

DISSOLVE TO

EXT NIGHT QUAY

Jimbo sits on a large mooring cleat holding a coconut. There

is no one else around. He slams the coconut on the cleat

splitting the thick husk. He tears the husk from the nut

as Mitch pulls up in an open jeep. Mitch takes out a folding

knife and opens the marlin spike. He hands it to Jimbo.

Jimbo uses the spike to puncture two holes in the husk and

hands the nut to Mitch to drink.Mitch moves into the

passenger seat.

                        MITCH

          Here's to the beginning of a wonderful

          friendship.

Mitch toasts with the nut, drinks and hands it back to Jimbo

who does the same.Jimbo gets in behind the wheel.

                        JIMBO

          Where are we going?

                        MITCH

          To the airport.

                        JIMBO

          The airport? It's closed at night. There

          won't be anybody there.

                        MITCH

          I hope you're right.

The jeep pulls away into the night.

EXT NIGHT ROAD

A pair of headlights move around the hills and through the

trees. The SOUND of the motor and the night creatures can be
heard. The sky is clear, full of stars.

EXT NIGHT AIRPORT

The terminal is a long low white building. A circular
driveway is in front of the open, deserted entrance. There
is no sign of life anywhere. Jimbo and Mitch pull up to the
entrance in the jeep.When it stops, Mitch jumps out. He puts
on a baseball cap and a pair of sunglasses and goes through
the entrance.

                              MITCH
                    Keep it running.

INT NIGHT AIRPORT

Inside are rows of plastic seats bolted to the floor. All
the lights are on. There is a long deserted ticket counter
with the names of airlines on the wall behind it. Across
from the counter is a row of shops, some with showcase
windows lit. At the far end of the seats TWO MEN sit with a
bucket and mop in front of them. One man is asleep on his
seat. The other is smoking and staring into the bucket.

Mitch enters quietly and goes to the front of the gift shop.
In the display window are rows of expensive watches.

Mitch looks at the two men at the far end of the terminal.
They are oblivious to him. He could be invisible.

Mitch sets himself in front of the display window with his
feet apart and his fists held waist high in front of him.
He takes a slow deep breath inward. The air bursts from his

lips in a loud puff. His left fist pulls back swiftly and

the right thrusts forward striking the window that shatters

and falls. The SOUND of an alarm bell goes off.Mitch quickly

grabs two handfuls of watches and is moving away as the two

men take notice of the commotion.

EXT NIGHT AIRPORT

Mitch tosses the watches on the floor of the jeep as he

jumps in. Jimbo is stunned.

                              JIMBO

                 What the hell!!

                              MITCH

                 Step on it. Now!

As they pull away from the terminal with a squeal of rubber,

an Island COP comes around the corner of the building.He

sees the fleeing taillights and goes cautiously inside.

EXT NIGHT ROAD

The jeep moves through the darkness under the starlit sky.

                              JIMBO (OFF CAMERA)

                 Did anybody see you?

                              MITCH (OFF CAMERA)

                 Two islanders. They'll each take a watch

                 for themselves and say they were in the

                 head when it happened.All they saw was a

                 yankee in a ball cap anyway.

INT NIGHT CAR

Mitch tosses out the ball cap and Jimbo drives.Mitch looks

up at the stars.

                            MITCH

            Beautiful clear night isn't it?

                            JIMBO

            Is this really the time for stargazing?

                            MITCH (emphatic)

            Turn off the headlights.

Jimbo reluctantly does as he's told. Mitch watches the sky.

POV MITCH

EXT NIGHT SKY

The stars shine brightly through the trees.

                                MITCH (OFF CAMERA)

                Slow. Slowly.Ready, right turn.Slower.

                Ready turn. Ready. Now. Hard Right.

EXT NIGHT ROAD

They turn hard right and the SOUND of it crashing through

the palm fronds and brush is heard abve thenight sounds.

                                MITCH (OFF CAMERA)

                ...two, three, four, ready stop.Now.

INT NIGHT CAR

Jimbo slams on the brakes and the car stops. Jimbo and Mitch

sit qietly for a minute feeling the draining of the adrenal

rush. They both laugh quietly.

                            MITCH

            My Uncle Sam taught me a lot of

            carryover skills besides diving.

                            JIMBO

            Like celestial navigation?

                         MITCH

The element of surprise ....

                         JIMBO

But what if that cop had been there...

                         MITCH

I was born to stay alive.Here, you're

good crew.

Mitch hands Jimbo a large silver watch with a luminous dial.

                         JIMBO

Wow, that's the best dive watch made.

                         MITCH

Just don't wear it on this island. Now,

let's bury the rest of this stuff. Six

months from now, we'll go down island

and be able live like kings. You've got

to think of the future.

                         JIMBO

I think I'd rather dive two hundred

feet for black coral.

                       MITCH (serious)

We all take something, don't we? We do

what we have to do to remain in

paradise. We're all pirates.

Jimbo takes his backpack from the back seat and puts the

watch inside. He puts it back behind the seat.

EXT NIGHT ROCK

Mitch and Jimbo get out of the jeep. Mitch takes a large

plastic bag and a folding shovel from under the seat.

Mitch puts the watches from the floor of the jeep into the bag.

Jimbo walks around to the front of the car and bumps into

a boulder. He measures the distance between the front of the

car and the rock. It is less than the length of his arms.

Jimbo shakes his head in disbelief and lets out a long sigh.

                        JIMBO

          Do you know how close we came? We could

          have been killed.

   Mitch comes around the car with the bag and the shovel. He

hands the shovel to Jimbo.

                        MITCH

          If you're not taking a chance, you're

          not having any fun.

EXT DAY QUAY

The quay is busy as before, natives and dock life

continuing. A taxi pulls away leaving Annie standing in

front of the Non-Select. She wears bright summer fashions

and holds a big floppy hat on against the wind with one

hand. She juggles a purse, camera bag and small suitcase

with the other hand trying to keep things together while

she searches for a familiar face. Jimbo comes out of the

Non-Select carrying his backpack and a speargun. He spots

Annie at the same time she spots him. There is a look of
relief on Annie's face. There is delightful surprise on
Jimbo's face.

> ANNIE (calls)
>
> Jim. Jimbo. I made it.

Jimbo comes over and awkwardly hugs her and her baggage.

> JIMBO
>
> Annie. You look great. You're so much
> more beautiful than I remembered that
> I hardly recognized you.

> ANNIE
>
> I was worried when I didn't see you at
> the airport.

> JIMBO
>
> Down here it's so easy to lose track of
> time.

Jimbo shows her that he doesn't wear a watch. He picks up
her suitcase. Annie takes off her watch and puts it away.

> ANNIE (excited)
>
> That's the way I want to be. It's so
> hard to believe that I'm finally here.
> I can't wait to get to the boat.

> JIMBO
>
> Relax. First I want you to see this
> unbelievable diving dog.

They go into the Non-Select.

INT DAY BAR

Mitch is at his usual place at the bar with his cat and
glass of lime water.Jimbo and Annie enter from the quay
entrance. They come around to Mitch. At the street entrance,
Dee is talking to the Island Cop.

                                    MITCH (smiles)

You must be Annie.

                                    JIMBO

This is Mitch. He's the captain of the

boat.

                                    MITCH

Jimbo has told me so much about you.

Jimbo makes a pained face behind Annie's back. Annie shakes
Mitch's hand and sits down between him and Jimbo. She sees
the cat and reaches out to pet it. The cat swipes at her.

                                    ANNIE

What a cute cat! What's his name,

Hitler?

                                    MITCH

His name is ......Pus n' Boots.

Jimbo whistles a sigh of relief.

                                    ANNIE

Just like the children's story. My

mother used to read it to me when I was

a kid. He's not very polite.

                                    MITCH (scolds)

Bad, pussy.

                        JIMBO

        Look, here comes the boat with the dog.

POV JIMBO

EXT DAY HARBOR

The blue boat with the black man and the black dog comes in

to anchor as before. The man goes forward on deck. The dog

follows.

INT DAY BAR

Jimbo and Annie look at the harbor. Mitch strokes the cat.

Dee comes back behind the bar and the Cop comes up behind

them.

                        JIMBO

            This is great, Annie. Wait till you see

            it. The dog really dives.

                        MITCH

            That's not so great is it, Pus?

                        ANNIE (delighted)

            This is all so unreal. Am I really here?

            I feel like I've escaped from somewhere.

                        COP

            What you got in the bag?

Annie's look of delight quickly changes to terror.

                        ANNIE

            Oh, no!

                        COP

            Not you, missy. I'm talking to the long

            haired boy. What's in the bag, mon?

Jimbo turns in his chair and holds his backpack in front of

him. Mitch looks straight ahead. Annie is relieved but

shaken.

                         JIMBO

          It's just my gear. What's the problem?

                         COP

          Somebody robbed the terminal gift shop

          last night.You be new on the island boy.

          Open the bag, mon.

Jimbo places the bag on the counter and unzips it next to

Annie. He takes out a dive mask and puts it down.

                         ANNIE(upset)

          Jimbo, I saw it at the airport. They

          broke a window....

Jimbo takes Annie's hand in his to comfort her .

                         JIMBO

          Don't worry bout a ting. Watch the guy

          on the boat. He'll dive in to check the

          anchor and the dog will dive after him.

Jimbo holds her wrist and with the other hand he points to

the harbor.

POV JIMBO

EXT DAY HARBOR

The black man dives from the bow of the boat and the dog

dives after him. One black head disappears beneath the

surface and then the other follows.

INT DAY BAR

Annie watches the harbor. Mitch watches Jimbo's hands. The
Cop looks out at the harbor.

                         COP

              Crazy fucken fisherman and his crazy

              fucken dog. I seen it plenty. It is a

              sight, missy. The bag, mon.

Jimbo takes his hand from Annie's wrist and she is wearing
the big dive watch. Annie covers the watch with her hat.

                         ANNIE

              Unbelievable! Crazy fucken dog!

                         MITCH

              Just show him the bag, Houdini.

                         COP

              (to Mitch) You know this long haired

              fucken Italian boy?

Mitch nods yes and the Cop quickly looks inside the bag and
gives it back to Jimbo.

                         ANNIE

              Where's the dog? Where's the fucken dog?

Everyone is now looking at the harbor.

POV ANNIE

EXT DAY HARBOR

The blue boat swings slowly at anchor. The head of the black
man is seen above the surface looking around, searching. He
dives under the surface again.

INT DAY BAR

Annie is hanging on to Jimbo's arm. Mitch is holding the
cat.Dee looks at them with a worried expression. The Cop
goes out onto the quay.

                         JIMBO

          He'll come up.

                         MITCH

          He always comes up last.

                         DEE

          But never this long.

EXT DAY QUAY

Jimbo and Annie come out of the bar after the Cop. Jimbo
slows Annie so that they lag behind.

                         ANNIE

          Thanks for the watch.

                         JIMBO

          It's a long story.

                         ANNIE

          At first, I thought he was after me.

                         JIMBO

          I think we have a lot to talk about.

A crowd has gathered at one spot on the wharf. Jimbo and
Annie wait at the edge. The Cop clears a way through the
crowd. The black man from the boat is soaking wet as he
walks past them with the wet lifeless black dog in his arms.

                        JIMBO

         (to the black man) What happened?

                      BLACK MAN

         Bad day for the dog, mon.

EXT DAY OCEAN

ESTABLISHING SHOT

The trimaran sails on the open sea. There are great white
puffy clouds in the bright blue sky. The sails are full and
the dinghy has been stowed on deck.

EXT DAY BOAT

Annie is seated in the cockpit. She doesn't look well. She
wears a long sleeved shirt, sunglasses and her hat tied on
with a string. Jimbo is forward winching the mainsail. He
wears only a brief bathing suit. Mitch is at the wheel in
shorts and tee shirt. His blue cap with the diving helmet
insignia is on the compass binnacle in front of him. Jim
comes back to the cockpit. He looks at Annie and then at
Mitch.

                        MITCH

         Bad day for the dog, mon.

                        JIMBO

         I can't figure out what went wrong.

                        ANNIE

         Do you believe in karma?

                        JIMBO

         Your karma or mine

                         MITCH
          I believe in the almighty and the
          almighty dollar.
Mitch puts out his hand palm up and Jimbo slaps it.
                         ANNIE
          I don't feel well.
                         JIMBO
          If you get sick, go in the net.
Jimbo points to the net between the hulls.Annie looks.
POV ANNIE
As the boat cuts through the water, waves wash up through
the net strung between the hulls.
                         JIMBO (OFF CAMERA)
          It flushes automatically and can be
          used as a bidet.
EXT DAY BOAT
Annie groans. Mitch looks at her sympathetically.
                         MITCH
          Jimbo, take the wheel.
Jimbo takes over at the helm and Mitch goes through the
companionway at the front of the cockpit.
INT DAY BOAT
Mitch swings down through the companionway without using the
ladder. To his left is a galley, to the right is a chart
table. Forward are bunks to the right and left. Far forward
is a large vee berth. The cat is on the bunk to the right
along with Annies bags.

                           MITCH

                (to cat) Excuse me, Pus.

Mitch moves the cat aside and moves the camera bag to get at
the purse. He opens the purse and finds a sheaf of travelers
checks. He shows the checks to the cat.

                                MITCH (cont.)

                She's got good karma and lots of it.

Mitch places the travelers checks back in the purse and
restores the bunk. The cat swipes at him. Mitch goes to the
galley and gets a can from an overhead storage compartment.
He takes out a brown hard shelled fruit, replaces the can
and goes back up top.

EXT DAY BOAT

Mitch comes up to the cockpit. Jimbo is still at the wheel.
Annie has her eyes closed and sits in a corner.

                           JIMBO

                What have you got, tamarind?

Mitch nods yes and peels the dark brown skin from the fruit
revealing a large seed covered by a juicy orange flesh.

                                MITCH (to Annie)

                Suck on this. It's a local remedy.

Annie opens her eyes and looks at Mitch and then sees the
fruit. She takes it and puts it in her mouth.

                                ANNIE (makes a face)

                It's so bitter. Is it poison? Please.

                Put me out of my misery.

Mitch gets behind Annie and puts his hands around her neck.

                         ANNIE

        Wait.I wasn't serious.

                         JIMBO

        Go easy on her.

                         MITCH

        Relax Annie.

Mitch presses his thumbs at the base of her skulls and very

slowly moves them down the back of her neck. With the same

deliberation he does the same thing to her shoulders.

                              ANNIE (sings softly)

        I like a man with a slow hand

        da da da dum with an easy touch.

                         JIMBO

        You're on the right boat.

                         ANNIE

        Oh, don't stop. (licks lips) This stuff

        really works.

                         JIMBO

        Some people have a need for speed. I'm a

        diver. I like to do things real slow.

                         MITCH

        The slower you go, the longer you can

        stay down.

Mitch reaches out his hand and Jimbo slaps it.

                              ANNIE (weak)

        Oh, never stop.

                              JIMBO (to Mitch)

        I can do that.

Jimbo and Mitch exchange place at the wheel and at Annie.

                         ANNIE

          What is this? Am I going to be your love

          slave.

                         MITCH

          It's your charter.

Annie relaxes again under Jimbo's hands. She is too drained

to resist anything.

                         ANNIE

          Oh, make me well, Jimbo. I think you

          two are my slaves.

                         MITCH

          How slow can you go.

                         JIMBO

          It's a good life, somebody has to live

          it.

Mitch and Jimbo both laugh. Annie regains a little strength.

                         ANNIE (to Mitch)

          So you're a diver too?

Mitch points to his insignia cap on the binnacle.

                         MITCH

          From the old school.

                         JIMBO

          UDT. Underwater Demolition Team.

                         ANNIE

          Should I be impressed?

JIMBO

Our karma is better than your karma.

MITCH (serious)

Jimbo, get the glasses.

Jimbo jumps from behind Annie and goes to the cabin . He reaches inside and brings out a pair of binoculars and hands them to Mitch. Mitch braces against the wheel and focuses the glasses.

MITCH

Eleven o clock low.

JIMBO

Looks like big turtle.

Annie gets up and comes next to them squeezing in between.

ANNIE

Where? Where is it? I want to see.

Jimbo points far ahead of them to a small brown spot in the water. It bobs up and down in the distance.

JIMBO

It looks like a head. Maybe it's a body.

ANNIE

Oh, no!

Mitch focuses the glasses and a wide smile comes to his lips.

MITCH

Thar she blows. Get out your speargun Jimbo. Square grouper off the starboard bow.

Jimbo excitedly lets out a loud whoop and rushes below.

                          ANNIE

                What's a square grouper?

                          MITCH (beams)

                Darling Annie, you sweet innocent child.

                A square grouper is a bale of marijuana.

                Fifty kilos. One hundred and ten pounds.

                And in these wayward islands, it is

                better than travelers checks. This is our

            lucky day.

Jimbo comes back on deck with his speargun loaded. He is

ready for business. He looks all around three hundred and

sixty degrees at the horizon. At the stern, he stops.

                          JIMBO

                There's a trawler, starboard quarter.

                He's closing.

Jimbo points aft. Mitch and Annie look.

POV ANNIE

EXT DAY OCEAN

Behind them in the distance is a large white power boat with

a high bow headed in their direction.

EXT DAY BOAT

Mitch turns back to steering toward the bale. Jimbo keeps an

eye aft. Annie looks forward to the left and points.

                          ANNIE

                Looks like bad weather.

POV ANNIE

EXT DAY OCEAN

Far ahead to the left is a dark storm cloud.

EXT DAY BOAT .

Mitch steers the boat. Annie stands next to him looking from
the storm to the trawler. Jimbo checks his speargun.

                    MITCH
          That storm is good weather for us.
          Jimbo, well take that bale on the port
          side.

                    JIMBO
          Aye aye.

Jimbo goes forward to the front of the net between the hulls
on the left side. He kneels with the speargun next to him.
As the boat rides the water splashes up in his face. He
enjoys it.

                    ANNIE (to Mitch)
          What about the trawler? What can I do?

Mitch hands Annie the binoculars and pulls in on the jib
sheet as he continues to steer.

                    MITCH (calm)
          Keep an eye on that boat. Let me know if
          you see any guns. And stay out of the
          way.

Annie moves back to her place in the corner and uses the
binoculars.

                    ANNIE (nervous)

He's still heading this way, but he

isn't gaining very fast. He's too far

to see details.

                    MITCH

If we can get into that storm, we can

outrun him.

                    ANNIE

In a sailboat?

                    MITCH

This is a trimaran sweetheart. We can go

as fast as the wind. (to Jimbo) Jimbo,

I'm going to tack after you shoot, watch

out for the sail coming across.

Jimbo salutes and picks up his gun. Annie looks through the

glasses.

                    ANNIE (worried)

He's gaining on us.

EXT DAY OCEAN

The trimaran approaches the bale.

EXT DAY BOAT

Jimbo waits on the net with his knees braced.

POV JIMBO

EXT DAY OCEAN

The distance between the boat and the bale decreases faster

and faster. The bow moves up and down in the waves that

splash up over the deck. the bale grows larger. It is brown

and wet bobbing like a cork in the waves.

EXT DAY BOAT

Mitch steers carefully to catch the bale between the hulls
in front of Jimbo. Jimbo fires the speargun. Mitch turns the
wheel. Jimbo is holding on to the gun leaning over the front
of the net. The spear sticking up from the bale rises up
toward Jimbo as a wave lifts it. Jimbo straightens up to
avoid the spear. The sail comes whipping across the bow
catching Jimbo in the back and knocking him forward into
the water. Annie screams.

                    MITCH (shouts)
          Annie, take the wheel. Aim for the
          storm.

Mitch jumps out of the cockpit and goes to the stern of the
portside outer hull. Annie takes the wheel. She looks
ahead.

POV ANNIE

EXT DAY OCEAN

The storm is very close and dead ahead.

EXT DAY BOAT

Annie looks to her left. Mitch is holding onto one of the
backstays. As Jimbo slides by between the hulls, he is
holding onto the speargun with both hands. The bale is on
the spear ahead of him. Mitch reaches down as Jimbo passes
and catches him by his long hair. Jim screams. The wind
picks up. Annie turns back to the storm. She is steady at
the wheel. It starts to rain.

EXT DAY OCEAN

The trimaran is screaming through the storm putting out a
large wake. Mitch is hanging off the stern pulling Jimbo
aboard by his head. Jimbo is hanging on to the bale.

EXT DAY BOAT

Annie steers through the storm.Mitch is still struggling
with Jimbo and the bale.

                    MITCH (yells)

          Fall off, Annie, fall off the wind.

Annie turns the wheel and the boat slows. A big wave passes
under them and as it rises Mitch lifts Jimbo onto the port
net. He and Jimbo pull the bale aboard. Mitch comes back
to the cockpit, wet and out of breath.

                    MITCH

          Annie, go help Jimbo.

Mitch takes the wheel from Annie and she works her way
carefully back to Jimbo as the fury of the storm increases.
She almost falls overboard blown by the wind but Jimbo
catches her. He seats her next to the bale and she holds
on to it while Jimbo gets a line from a stern cleat and
begins lashing the bale to the boat.

                    ANNIE (proudly)

          I remembered everything you taught me.

Jimbo smiles and ties a rope around her waist as a big wave
washes over them. He holds on to her tightly. She lets
herself be held.

                           JIMBO

          How do you feel, Annie?

                           ANNIE (smiles)

          Great. (she spits out the seed)

          That stuff really works. I'm not sick

          anymore.

EXT DAY OCEAN

The trimaran flies through the storm and disappears.

DISSOLVE TO

EXT DAY BAY

The trimaran hangs at anchor in a crescent shaped bay. There

are high rocky cliffs at both ends of the crescent. In the

middle is a small sandy beach in front of thick vegetation

that covers the island. There are birds and bright flowers

everywhere. Mitch is on the bow of the boat and Jimbo is in

front of him in the water.

EXT DAY BOAT

Mitch lets out the anchor rode and then ties it off. He

looks over the bow to Jimbo in the water.

                           MITCH

          How's it hangen?

                           JIMBO

          Real good . I buried the anchor.

Annie comes from the cabin with a towel and a bottle of

sunscreen. She wears a bikini and sunglasses. She comes

forward near Mitch.

                                MITCH

                Jimbo, while you're wet, why don't you

                hunt us up something to eat. (looks over

                and grins at Annie) What would you

                like, skipper?

                                ANNIE (quickly)

                Lobster, lobster and lobster.

                                MITCH (salutes Annie)

                Aye aye.

Mitch goes to the cockpit to fetch a net bag. Annie leans

over the bow.

                                ANNIE

                I love it. The water is so clean and

                clear.

                                JIMBO

                Welcome to paradise.

Mitch returns with bag which he tosses to Jimbo who catches

it and slips beheath the surface. While Annie fixes herself

for sunbathing on the bow, Mitch rigs a tarpaulin over the

cockpit and also shades the bale still tied to the net

between the hulls. He talks to Annie as he works.

                                MITCH

                You were good at the wheel. You make

                good crew.

                                ANNIE

                Jimbo taught me when I learned to dive.

                (looks at surrounding hills) This

                is incredible! Does it have a name?

                    MITCH

Money Bay. The island is the one Robert

Louis Stevenson visited before he wrote

Treasure Island.

                    ANNIE

Money Bay. (sighs) I never thought I'd

wind up here.

                    MITCH

What's all this karma crap? Did you kill

somebody?

                    ANNIE

You might as well know. (looks at the

bale) I guess I can tell you now. The

money I gave you to pay for this charter

was obtained from an insurance fraud.

                    MITCH

You don't say! (stares at Annie) Who'd

have thunk it?

                    ANNIE (serious)

What goes around....

                    MITCH (interrupts)

goes around.

                    ANNIE

I have a lot of guilt. Jewish blood

on my father's side. I really didn't

do it.

                    MITCH

I believe you.

>   ANNIE (insistent)
> My ex-boyfriend did it. Everything I
> declared was really taken, except for my
> camera and that was at my mother's and
> I forgot that I left it there.

>   MITCH (declares)
> Innocent.

>   ANNIE
> No. I'm serious.

>   MITCH
> I'm serious too. Out here, on this boat,
> I make the law.

>   ANNIE
> When that cop came up behind me at the
> Non-Select, I almost had a heart attack.
> I knew everyone on the plane was looking
> at my camera bag. It's silly. Did you
> ever read Crime and Punishment?

>   MITCH
> I only read the first half. Crime.

>   ANNIE (laughs)
> You are too too much.

After Mitch ties off the last corner of the awning at the
stern, he takes a beach towel from the cockpit, ties it to
the boat and lets it hang into the water. He then comes up
to Annie who turns from her back onto her stomach.

> MITCH
>
> Don't get more than ten minutes on each
> side the first day.

Mitch picks up the sunscreen and begins rubbing it on
Annie's back.

> ANNIE
>
> Why did you hang the towel in the water,
> in case of lightening?
>
> MITCH
>
> No. That's for Pus. So when he goes for
> a swim, he can claw his way back onto
> the boat.

Annie gives a look of disbelief at being put on and turns her head
away from Mitch. He unhooks the top to her bikini.

> ANNIE
>
> What are you doing!
>
> MITCH
>
> We're in International waters. You can
> go topless here.
>
> ANNIE
>
> I've been to the French islands. I'm not
> naive as you may think.

Mitch rubs the lotion on the back of her legs up to her
buttocks.

> MITCH
>
> You're in great shape.

                        ANNIE

        Thank you. I work at it. Do you have a

        law against wearing a bottom?

                        MITCH

        No. It's better if some part of you is

        white.

                        ANNIE

        Why's that?

                        MITCH

        That way it's easier to find you in the

        dark.

Mitch smacks her bottom, not hard but loud. Annie jumps up
and redoes her top.

                        ANNIE

        I think I'll cool off.

Annie dives into the clear water. Mitch goes to a hatch in
the outer hull and takes out a mask and snorkle and a pair
of fins. He tosses them to Annie in the water.

                        MITCH

        You know how to use these. (looks around

        the bay and points) Jimbo is over

        by those rocks.

                        ANNIE (smiles)

        Thanks. (putting on the mask) I'm a

        diver too.

Annie pulls down the mask and with a kick of her fins slides
beneath the surface.

EXT DAY UNDERWATER

Annie is at home underwater, her slow graceful movements
flow with the waving seafans and soft finger corals. She
swims under the boat and sees a large baracuda waiting
there. She is not afraid. Annie swims through a school of
small fish that scatter like a shattered rainbow. Annie
swims down to a coral ledge and holds on to watch an
angelfish that watches her. Annie kicks her way to the
surface.

EXT DAY BAY

Annie's head pops above the surface and she grabs a deep
fast breath of air. She looks off toward the rocks.

POV ANNIE

EXT DAY BAY

At the base of the rock cliffs near the beach in the
crescent a pair of flippers kick and disappear.

EXT DAY UNDERWATER

Annie dives down and begins to swim. She takes in all the
beautifully colored life on the reefs and sand. She surfaces
but continues looking down and around, breathing through
her snorkle. She notices the baracuda following her.

POV ANNIE

EXT DAY UNDERWATER

Annie keeps looking back at the baracuda but continues to
swim calmly. Beneath her she sees Jimbo hanging on to an old
rope attached to an old anchor as he watches a lobster's
antennae beneath a ledge. He looks up and see her.

EXT DAY UNDERWATER

Annie points to the baracuda still the same distance behind

her. Jimbo kicks up to her carrying a bag full of lobsters.

EXT DAY BAY

Jimbo and Annie talk on the surface.

> ANNIE
>
> I know they don't bother divers but he's
>
> been following me ever since I left the
>
> boat.

> JIMBO
>
> Don't worry. They're like dogs. They'll
>
> follow you everywhere but won't get
>
> any closer unless you have fish. If they
>
> see you shoot a speargun, they always
>
> stay just out of range.

> ANNIE
>
> I remember what you taught me about
>
> them, but they look so menacing.

> JIMBO
>
> Get used to him. He'll live under the
>
> boat until we leave eating our scraps
>
> or whatever comes to feed on them. He's
>
> our pet baracuda now. Follow me.

EXT DAY UNDERWATER

Jimbo dives down followed by Annie. They both wave to the

baracuda who looks at them and follows. Jimbo swims down

under a large boulder and up through a shaft of light on

the other side. Annie follows him.

INT DAY CAVE

Jimbo and Annie surface in a pool in the center of a small
cave. They are completely surrounded by rocks but for an
opening in the roof that lets in a shaft of sunlight.

                         ANNIE (aghast)

          This is fantastic!

                         JIMBO

               Come on.

Jimbo leads Annie onto the rocks. They take off their dive
gear and relax. Jimbo puts the bag of lobsters aside. Jimbo
moves in next to Annie who is lays out on a rock in the
sunlight. She takes off her top. Jimbo lies next to her with
his face close to hers.

                         ANNIE

               I never expected a place so, so....

                         JIMBO

               romantic.

Annie looks at him and smiles.

                         ANNIE

               In the poetic sense. (laughs) Don't

               pout. I had such a crush on you when you

               were giving us lessons. But you were

               more interested in my friend I guess

               it was that black dress...

                         JIMBO (realizes)

               low cut in the back. And you were the

               one with the braces on her teeth.

ANNIE

Look. No more braces.

Jimbo kisses her on the lips . When she doesn't resist, he
kisses her more passionately and caresses her. He whispers
in her ear.

JIMBO

You are so beautiful.

ANNIE

Did you really think about me every day?

Jimbo ignores the question and kisses her again. They both
laugh.

JIMBO

I will now.

He kisses her slowly along her arm, across her chest and
down her bare belly to her bikini bottom.

ANNIE (groans)

I wish I had brought some condoms.

JIMBO

What!

ANNIE

Condoms. Aren't you worried about who
I've been sleeping with?

JIMBO (breathless)

I don't care about that.

Annie sits and straightens herself.

ANNIE

In that case, I'm worried about you.

                                    JIMBO

                    We'd better get back to the boat while

                    the lobsters are still fresh.

EXT DAY BOAT .

Mitch can be seen in the galley taking broiled lobsters out

of the oven. Jimbo is positioning the bale in the center

of the cockpit and Annie has a red checkered tablecloth to

cover it.

                                    ANNIE (smells food)

                    That is divine. (looks around) This is

                    heaven. Now I know why my mother made

                    me say all those Our Fathers and Hail

                    Marys.

Mitch comes up from the galley with a tray of lobsters and

three wooden plates.

                                    MITCH (to Annie)

                    Between a Catholic mother and a Jewish

                    father no wonder you're so screwed up.

                                    ANNIE

                    What do you mean by that?

                                    JIMBO

                    He's just teasing you. Eat something,

                    maybe you won't feel so paranoid.

Mitch goes back down and comes up with a bowel of rice, a

bowel of greens and some silverware. Annie has a lobster

in front of her.

                            MITCH

          Wait. Always first piece for the cat.

Mitch cuts a piece and holds it by the cabin door luring the

cat on deck. .

                            JIMBO

          This is how we check for poison.

Mitch and Jimbo laugh. The cat swipes at the piece of

lobster-- . Mitch tosses back off the stern.

                            ANNIE

          You two have a rotten sense of humor.

The cat runs aft and dives after the piece of lobster. Annie

does a double take. So does Jimbo.

                            MITCH

          What diving dog?

Mitch goes aft and pulls up the towel with the cat clinging

to it . The cat jumps onto the deck and goes off to chew on

the peice of lobster in its mouth. Mitch sits down with

Jimbo and Annie who are still stunned in disbelief. They

pass around the plates and food and begin to eat.

                            MITCH

          Nice table.

                            JIMBO

          I didn't want it to get spotted. In case

          anybody dropped by.

Annie savors her lobster. She swallows and talks.

                            ANNIE

          I know this is all very illegal.

                              MITCH

          I told you those laws don't apply to us.

                              ANNIE

          They've been seizing boats in

          International waters. It's been in all

          the papers.

                              MITCH

          I don't read the papers. We can defend

          ourselves.

                              JIMBO

          I've got speargun, and a slingshot in

          my bag.

                              MITCH

          There's a shotgun under my bunk and a

          .45 automatic under my pillow.

                              ANNIE

          Whoa. I don't know if I want any part of

          this.

                              MITCH

          You wouldn't be the first tourist lost at

          sea.

                              JIMBO

          He's only kidding.

Mitch laughs and then Jimbo laughs. Annie sees that they're

joking rough again and she shakes her head and laughs with

them.

                              ANNIE

          Please. Just let me enjoy my last meal.

Mitch and Jimbo laugh with her.

JIMBO

The last thing I read in the paper was
that doctors had found that marijuana
good for high blood pressure, glaucoma,
and a bunch of other diseases.

MITCH

It's also good getting stoned.

JIMBO

Oh, no, no, no. That part is bad for
you. They want to synthesize it so that
you get all the benefits except " the
euphoric effect."

MITCH

It's legal as long as it doesn't make
you feel good. That's why I live on a
boat. You can get drugs if a
psychiatrist prescribes it, uppers,
downers, sideways.

JIMBO

I guess you got to be crazy to get
drugs. Or rich.

MITCH

I'll bet this table has a street value
of a hundred grand.

JIMBO

If we roll it into joints. Have you got
a thousand dollars worth of papers.

                         MITCH

No. I don't smoke.

                         JIMBO

    Me too. What about a pipe. No? No.

                         ANNIE

This is great. Fantastic. I'm on a boat

where no one smokes. Fresh air. I love

it. (to Jimbo and Mitch) I've got

twelve boxes of brownie mix.

EXT DAY BOAT

The sun is setting in the background filling the sky with

color. Jimbo is on the stern with his slingshot. The table

is cleared and Mitch is readying a lantern. Annie is in the

galley cooking.

                         ANNIE

    Jimbo said buy what you want to eat.

    So I bought rice, vegetables and brownie

    mix.

                         MITCH

Twelve boxes!

                         ANNIE

    If I had known you two wanted some, I'd

    have bought more.

Mitch lifts the corner of the tablecloth and takes his

rigging knife out. He cuts into the corner of the bale.

                         JIMBO

    Want to bet I can hit that brown booby

    in the butt?

Annie comes up on deck. She goes back to Jimbo who is aiming
the sligshot.

POV ANNIE

EXT DAY BAY .

The colors of the sky are reflected in the water. On a
partially submerged rock near the shore, a brown bird sits
drying its spread wings. Next to the rock floats an old
white clorox bottle.

EXT DAY BOAT

Annie pushes past Mitch.She reaches for Jimbo just as he
lets the shot fly.

                                    ANNIE (pleading)

                    Jimbo! NO!

The SOUND of a loud POP.

POV ANNIE

EXT DAY BAY

The clorox bottle jumps, the bird flies away and ripples
break up the reflected sunset.

EXT DAY BOAT

Annie smacks Jimbo on the arm and he laughs.

                         JIMBO

               And I was aiming at the bottle.

                         ANNIE

               You two are driving me crazy.

She hits Jimbo again. He puts his arm around her.

                         JIMBO

               Will you tie me to the mast later and

               whip me? (whispers) Mitch has some

               condoms in the cabin.

Mitch comes over to Annie with a large chunk of marijuana.

                    MITCH

          Don't worry, Annie. On my boat we only

          kill what we eat and only take what we

          need.

Jimbo takes the chunk and smells it.

                    JIMBO

          Or what Allah drops in our laps.

                    ANNIE

          Maybe we're just being tested.

                    MITCH

          My track record on temptation is well

          known. I always give in.

DISSOLVE TO

EXT NIGHT BOAT

The lantern on top of the bale is lit. Next to it is half a

cake pan of brownies and a lot of crumbs. Jimbo is in the

port net playing with the cat. Mitch is bringing stereo

speakers on deck through the forward hatch. Annie arches her

back and stretches against the mast. The moon has risen.

There is a towel hung on a line between the mast and the

boom. The wind whips it and its shadow disrupts the light

and shadows. The boat hardly moves on the water. Annie

looks up at the sky.

                    ANNIE (in a voice too

          loud) How long does it take this stuff

          to work?

                              MITCH (softly)

You'll know.

Annie begins her martial arts routine moving slowly around

the deck.

                              JIMBO

          Mitch, how are we going to split it?

                              MITCH

          The traditional way. One third for the

          boat. One third for the captain. One

          third for the crew.

Annie comes near Mitch. He joins her in the exercise. He

moves with her in the oriental choreography of self

discipline and self defense.

                              JIMBO

          Well, I'm going to split my third with

          Annie.

Annie stops the routine. Mitch continues.

                              ANNIE (surprised)

You're what!

                              JIMBO

          Half the crew share goes to you. Without

          you I'd be floating on a bale in the

          middle of the ocean.

                              ANNIE

You don't have to.

                              JIMBO

I want to do it.

Annie goes over to Jimbo in the net. She gets down and hugs
and kisses him.

                    ANNIE

          Jimbo, you're so good to me. I don't

          know how to thank you.

                    JIMBO (whispers)

          I can think of some way.

                    ANNIE (whispers)

          I just got my period.

                    JIMBO (disappointed)

          I'll take a rain check.

                    ANNIE (confidentially)

          What does he mean by one third for the

          boat? Isn't that the same as he.

                    JIMBO (openly)

          Every boat needs repairs, new paint, a

          bottom job....

                    MITCH

          Satellite navigation, auto steering,

          short wave radio.

Mitch moves over to the net. He stands over Annie and Jimbo.

                    ANNIE (troubled)

          The benefits of a life of crime.

                    MITCH (domineering)

          Go ahead,continue to live your life by a

          bunch of rules set down by fat old white

          men in country clubs.

Annie moves frightened into Jimbo's arms. He is cool to her.
Annie's behavior is exaggerated,her eyes glassy.

> ANNIE (timidly)
>
> It isn't legal.

> MITCH (evangelical)
>
> It was legal when my old man got drunk
> and fell down the steps and broke his
> neck. It was legal when my mother smoked
> cigarettes through a tube in her neck
> because she had throat cancer.Fuck them
> and fuck their laws. The only law on my
> boat is the law of the jungle.

> JIMBO
>
> Big fish eat little fish. That's why
> we're out here. That's why we're
> pirates. We don't want anybody running
> our lives.

> ANNIE (amazed)
>
> I'm in never never land. It's Peter Pan
> and the little boys won't grow up.

Mitch gets down close to Annie and she follows his hand as
he points to the sky.

> MITCH (smiles)
>
> First star to the right and straight on
> till morning.

Mitch puts out his hand and Annie slaps it. They all laugh.

Annie gets up and they follow her as she runs back to the cockpit. She rips the table cloth from the bale. She stands the bale with her feet apart. Mitch and Jimbo are at her feet to each side. Jimbo grabs one ankle. Mitch grabs the other.

                    MITCH (to Jimbo)

Make a wish.

Annie kneels down.

                    ANNIE (conspiratorially)

One hundred and ten pounds. One hundred fifty dollars an ounce. Sixteen ounces in a pound. How much?

                    MITCH

The boat gets a computer.

                    JIMBO

I want a new mask, new fins, new....

Annie stands and yells.

                    ANNIE

We're rich!

                    MITCH

I think the brownies have kicked in.

                    ANNIE (yells)

We're fucking rich!

EXT NIGHT BAY

The trimara sits all alone in the crescent under the full moon and under the stars. Annie's voice echos across the water between the hills.

                         ANNIE (OFF CAMERA)

              We are RICH!!!

DISSOLVE TO

EXT DAY BOAT ·

The brownie tray sits empty on top of the bale along with an

almost empty bag of cookies, an open bag of potatoe chips,

empty soda bottles etc... the debris of a giant bout of the

munchies. The cat is asleep on the cabin roof. Forward there

is a large open hatch and smaller open hatches above the

bunks in the main cabin. The cat looks up. The loud SOUND of

a large chain rattling and a large splash is heard. Mitch's

head pops up in the forward hatch. Jimbo's head comes up in

the port hatch. Annies head sticks out of the starboard

hatch. Annie and Jimbo look at each other with puffy eyes.

Mitch comes on deck through the forward hatch. He turns and

looks at Jimbo's and Annie's head and then looks forward.

                         MITCH

              So, you think we're rich, Annie?

Annie stares straight ahead.

POV ANNIE

EXT DAY BAY

The CAMERA TILTS UP from the bow of the trimaran across the

fifty yards of water in front of it to disclose a huge motor

yacht with a helicopter on the back setting its anchor in

front of them. As the anchor holds, the stern swings so that

it is hanging back toward the trimaran.

                              ANNIE (OFF CAMERA)

          (impressed) It's the mudderfucker.

DISSOLVE TO

EXT DAY YACHT·

Victoria is on the afterdeck. THREE CREWMEN work around her.

Victoria puts on a scarf and sunglasses looking over her

shoulder toward the trimaran. CREW 1 is climbing the

stairway to the helicopter pad above them. CREW 2 is

lowering the motorized tender from davits. CREW 3 comes

up to Victoria with a pair of binoculars.

                              VICTORIA

          Thank you. (takes glasses)

                              CREW 3

          We are going to get Mister Carl at the

          airport. We are preparing the tender.

          We are making escargot and champagne for

          lunch. Is there anything else that Missy

          desires?

Victoria looks through the binoculars at the trimaran.

POV VICTORIA

EXT DAY BOAT

Through the binoculars Victoria sees the two men and one

woman on the bow of the smaller boat, sitting looking back

at her. CAMERA ZOOMS in on the face of Annie, then Jimbo

and lingers on the face of Mitch.

MONEY BAY

EXT DAY BAY

The helicopter rises up from the yacht and passes over the trimaran.

EXT DAY BOAT

The shadow and the SOUND of the helicopter pass over Annie, Jimbo and Mitch as they sit in their swimsuits on the bow of the trimaran.

                    ANNIE
        When my ex-boyfriend got his first real
        acting job, we decided to take all our
        friends out to celebrate. We decided to
        get a limosine. The guy renting them
        says."Do you want the regular?" Nooo.
        "Do you want the stretch?" Nooo. We said
        we wanted the biggest one he had. He
        says, " Ohhh, you want the
        mudderfucker."

                    JIMBO
        Maybe it's a figment of the brownies.

                    MITCH
        They better not come over here.

                    ANNIE (smells something)
        Oh, no. They're cooking food. (to yacht)
        We were here first. Move out.

                    JIMBO
        Someones getting in the tender.

EXT DAY BAY

At the yacht, Crew 2 helps Victoria into the tender. She

settles herself. He casts off and heads toward the trimaran.

INT DAY BOAT .

Jimbo has his head up through his hatch. Annie is standing

in the cabin. Mitch is forward at the vee berth.

> JIMBO (calls down)
>
> One man in a uniform and someone behind
>
> him heading this way.

Mitch comes out of the vee berth with a shotgun.

> MITCH
>
> No matter what happens, nobody comes on
>
> board.

> ANNIE
>
> Wait a minute. Let's reconsider our
>
> options.

Jimbo pulls his head down and instructs Annie.

> JIMBO
>
> Annie, there's only one captain on this
>
> boat. That's Mitch.

> ANNIE
>
> You mean I have no say.

> MITCH
>
> It's not a democracy. Here's the plan...

Jimbo has his head back up the hatch.

> JIMBO (calls down)
>
> They've stopped half way here. Hold on.
>
> The one in the back is a woman.

                                    ANNIE (to Mitch)
                You're not afraid of a woman are you?

                                    MITCH
                All right, no guns. But still no one

                comes on board.

EXT DAY BAY

The tender has stopped half way to the trimaran. Mitch,Jimbo

and Annie come up on deck. Jimbo has the binoculars.

POV JIMBO

EXT DAY BAY

Through the binoculars, Jimbo sees Crew 2. The woman behind

him is looking at something in the water to the far side of

the tender. As she turns, Victoria looks straight at Jimbo.

                                    JIMBO (OFF CAMERA)
                    Well,la di da. It's that rich dame we

                    met at the Non-Select and her chauffeur.

EXT DAY BOAT

Jimbo continues to watch. Annie moves next to Mitch, who is

rigging a fender on the port side.

                                    ANNIE
                Some boat. She must be some woman. Can

                you imagine being on a boat like that.

                                    MITCH
                I wouldn't like being a chauffeur.

                                    JIMBO
                Here she comes.

EXT DAY BAY

The tender pulls with Victoria and Crew 2 pulls alongside

the trimaran where Annie , Mitch and Jimbo wait on the port

side.   ·

EXT DAY BOAT

Mitch takes a bow line from Crew 2. As the tender bounces

against the fender, the cat jumps soaking wet from

Victoria's lap onto the trimaran. Jimbo straightens the cloth

on of the bale in the cockpit. Annie stands next to Mitch.

                              VICTORIA (concerned)

                    We found him in the water near our boat.

                              MITCH (to Jimbo)

                    Jimbo, I thought I told you to tie a

                    rock to that cat.

                              ANNIE (to Victoria)

                    He's joking. The cat...

                              MITCH (interrupts)

                    must have fallen overboard. Thanks a lot

                    for saving his life.

Victoria tries to judge Mitch and looks over Annie before

responding.

                              VICTORIA

                    In that case,I'd like to invite you over

                    for dinner. We'll have lobster.

                              ANNIE

                    Oh no, not more lobster!

                              JIMBO

          We're divers. We could sell you

          lobsters.

                              VICTORIA (to Jimbo)

          I'll bet you could. (to Mitch) What

          about after dinner?

                              ANNIE

          For dessert?

                              VICTORIA

          We have ice cream.

                              MITCH

          I'll bet you have everything.

                              VICTORIA

          No one's ever been disappointed.

Mitch tosses the bow line back to Crew 2.

                              MITCH

          Dessert. Send the tender to pick us up

          after dark.

EXT DAY BAY

The tender with Victoria and Crew 2 drifts away from the

trimaran with Annie , Mitch and Jimbo. It's motor starts

and it heads back to the yacht.

EXT DAY BOAT

Annie, Mitch and Jimbo huddle in the cockpit.

                              ANNIE (to Mitch)

          Why didn't you tell her about Pus.

                              MITCH

          Never tell them everything.

                          ANNIE

          What's romance without mystery!

                          JIMBO (butts in)

          What are we going to do with the dope?

                          MITCH

          We'll wait till after dark. Here's the

          plan.

DISSOLVE TO

EXT DAY BOAT

Annie lays out in the sun on her towel with her top off.

Jimbo naps in the shaded net. Mitch sits in the shade of the

cockpit repairing a sail with a needle and yarn. The cat

sleeps on of the cloth covered bale. The day is hot and

clear. The SOUND of easy going Island music comes from the

stereo speakers on deck.

EXT DAY BAY

The SOUND of the Island music travels across the water from

the trimaran to the yacht.

EXT DAY YACHT

Victoria sits in a lounge chair on the after deck looking

back at the trimaran. She sips champagne from a glass. A

bucket stands next to her. Crew 3 puts the bottle into the

ice bucket and exits forward. Victoria closes her eyes

and smiles.

DISSOLVE TO

EXT NIGHT BOAT

Annie comes up from the cabin in a loose summer dress.

Jimbo is in the dinghy at the back of the boat and Mitch
is lowering the bail into the dinghy. They both wear bathing
suits. They work in the dark. The SOUND of the tender can
be heard coming closer. Jimbo pulls the dinghy up between
the hulls to conceal it. Annie goes to Mitch. Mitch touches
Annie's sunburnt shoulder .

                         MITCH

          Tssssss. You got some sun. I have some

          aloe to rub on it later.

                              ANNIE (gets chills)
          What should I tell her when you're not

          there.

                         MITCH

          You're a smart girl, you'll think of

          something. We'll be along after we stash

          the dope. Jimbo says there's a cave.

          We've got dry clothes in a plastic bag.

                         ANNIE

          Be careful.

The light from the tender sweeps across Annie and finds her.
She waves.

                         MITCH (smiles)

          If you can't be careful, be quick.

EXT NIGHT BAY

The tender driven by Crew 2 pulls up alongside the
trimaran.Annie gets in and they head toward the yacht.

INT NIGHT YACHT

The large salon is enclosed with glass that looks out on the afterdeck. Behind a wet bar, the interior wall holds animal trophies; the heads of a ram, a lion, a deer and a bear. To one side of the bar a small office space has been set up and Victoria sits at a computer busy with business. Crew 3 opens the exterior door from the deck and Annie enters. Victoria looks from her work.

                    VICTORIA
          Just let me finish this entry for
          tomorrow's trading. Make yourself at
          home.

Annie goes to a table across from the office. There are four place settings. She hesitates there. Then she forces herself to look at the trophies. She stops in front of the ram. Victoria comes up behind her.

                    ANNIE
          You know, this one is an endangered
          species.

                    VICTORIA
          I know very little about any of them. My
          husband likes trophies. It keeps him
          from shooting me.

                    ANNIE
          What does he expect to kill here?

                    VICTORIA
          Nothing. This is my idea. My first
          husband brought me here years ago.
          Where are the boys?

                              ANNIE

          They don't tell me anything. I'm just

          a woman.

                              VICTORIA

          We both know better than that, honey.

          But, I understand. My third husband

          was like that.

                              ANNIE

          First husband, third husband. How many

          have you had?

                              VICTORIA

          How many have had me. I'm from that

          generation that never slept with a man

          unless you were going to marry him. I've

          never been one to give it away.

Annie looks around at the luxury and returns to the table.

                              ANNIE

           I've never been one to sell it.

                              VICTORIA

          So, you're a philanthropist and I'm a

          .... a business woman.

Annie goes over and looks at the computer setup.

                              ANNIE

          You run your business from here? I

          work at home a lot too.

Victoria comes over to the desk and proudly shows Annie

her business operation.

                        VICTORIA

        We're in banking and investments. This

        machine keeps me in touch with the

        world. I'm very deliberate. I never make

        quick decisions. I like to go slow.

                        ANNIE

        Then you'll like the boys. They're

        divers. They say that the slower you

        go the longer you can stay down. How

        slow can you go?

Annie puts out her hand palm up. Victoria catches on quickly

and slaps it. They both laugh.

                        VICTORIA

        They do that a lot don't they.

Annie refers to the trophies.

                        ANNIE

        Is Mr. Macho going to join us?

                        VICTORIA

        The helicopter went to pick him up at

        the airport. He's been in Alaska

        shooting something big.

                        ANNIE

        And he left you here to run the store?

                        VICTORIA (definite)

        It's my store, honey. You've a nice *sense*

        of irony.

                        ANNIE

        Publishing. I'm a junior editor.

                         VICTORIA

     Do you love it ?

                          ANNIE

     I love the artistic part where you share

     knowledge and join in creation, but the

     business end....

                         VICTORIA

     It's an acquired taste.

The sound of a helicopter can be heard and they go to the

window.

POV ANNIE

EXT NIGHT BAY

Through the glass Annie can see the dinghy with Mitch and

Jimbo spotlighted by a light from the yacht. They have

stopped rowing and are looking up.

INT NIGHT HELICOPTER

Crew 1 sits next to CARL. Carl has a full white beard and

wears a bush jacket.

                          CARL

     Let's take a closer look at the company

     she's been keeping while I've been away.

EXT NIGHT BAY

Jimbo and Mitch are blinded by the light from the yacht. The

SOUND of the helicopter becomes deafening and the water

becomes churned up as the helicopter get closer. The dinghy

is swamped. Jimbo and Mitch are soaked.

DISSOLVE TO

INT NIGHT YACHT

Crew 3 is serving ice cream to Annie. Jimbo and Mitch sit

rapped in towels. Mitch wears his cap with the dive

insignia. Victoria gets up to greet Carl as he comes into

the room. Carl goes to the bar pours a big drink and gets

a big cigar.

                              CARL (to table)

          I hope I didn't scare you with that

          chopper stunt. That was pretty risky at

          night.

                              JIMBO

          We're used to the water.

                              MITCH

          If you're not taking a risk, you're

          not having any fun.

                              CARL (to Crew 3)

          I'm starving. How about a big lobster,

          lots of butter . Chop chop.

Crew 3 exits and Carl talks to Victoria ignoring the others.

                              VICTORIA

          You missed dinner.

                              CARL

          Did you hear about that Senate

          investigation of Savings and Loans?

                              VICTORIA

          We'll discuss it later.

Carl and Victoria come over to the table.

                            CARL (complains)

I missed getting a Kodiak bear in

Alaska this morning. I got a supeona in

D.C. this afternoon. I missed my

connection in Dallas and I missed dinner

with my lovely wife tonight.

                            MITCH

Bad day for the dog, mon.

                            JIMBO

What is the government after you for?

                            CARL

We put a lot of money into the S&Ls.

                            VICTORIA

They aren't interested, dear.

Carl lights his cigar and Annie discreetly gets up from the

table and takes her ice cream to the wet bar to eat. Annie

turns so that she can't see the trophies.

                            CARL (boasts)

And they loaned us (refers to Victoria)

or our corporations more than we put in.

This woman is amazing. She was voted one

of the top ten female executives by MS

magazine

                            MITCH

And then you defaulted on the loans and

the S&Ls failed and the government gave

you back the money you put in. (smiles

at Victoria) She's worth her weight in

Deposit Insurance. (winks at her)

My kind of gal.

                         VICTORIA

It's not that simple.

                         JIMBO (impressed)

.   More pirates in paradise, but for

millions.

                         ANNIE

Big time ripoff artists.

                         CARL

In for a penny, in for a pound. We're

going to buy this little island.

Annie looks around and comes over by Mitch.

                         ANNIE (to Mitch)

Is this where it all leads?

                         MITCH

Not for me. An old Greek told me. Don't

buy anything if it flies, floats or fucks.

Rent and leave big tips.

Jimbo and Carl laugh. Annie turns away. Victoria smiles.

                         VICTORIA

I think that's just talk. What about

your boat.

                         MITCH

It owns me. I'm just the caretaker. What

about you ? Are you owned or rented.

Everyone waits for Victoria to answer but she says nothing.

                         CARL (dominant)

Well what do you think of her? The boat.

MONEY BAY

JIMBO

Nice boat.

CARL

And my trophies. That fellow over there.

(points to bear head) He stood

thirteen feet high. Shot him with a dear

rifle. Cost a fortune to get.

ANNIE

I think it all stinks. Excuse me I need

some fresh air.

Annie gets up and exits to the outer deck. Victoria pushes
away her uneaten ice cream. Jimbo continues to eat . Mitch
stands up. Carl looks up at him.

CARL

And you, Mister Diver. What do you

think.

MITCH

I never killed anything bigger than a

man and I got paid to do that.

EXT NIGHT YACHT

Annie is standing against the stern rail looking back at the
trimaran. Mitch comes out and stands next to her.

ANNIE

Do you hate them as much as I do?

We were rude. I know it's wrong but

I wish somebody had shot him instead

of those innocent animals.

                        MITCH (philosophical)

Right? Wrong? Is he so much worse than

others? Uncle Sam pays you and you do it

and innocents die. It's legal and they

give you a medal. You do the same kind

of thing for a private contractor. Only

players who know the score get killed.

illegal, but the money. The money is so

much better.

                        ANNIE (resigned)

Crime pays.

Mitch starts to slowly rub the back of Annie's neck.

                        MITCH

Virtue is its own reward.

INT NIGHT YACHT

Jimbo is having a drink at the bar with Carl. Victoria is

looking out at the afterdeck.

                        JIMBO

Did you track him through the snow?

                        CARL (watching Victoria)

No. We sat in a blind drinking brandy.

We had baited a trap with something he

liked and when he came sniffing around,

I shot him.

                        JIMBO

I prefer swimming in warm water after

grouper.

                            CARL (to Jimbo)

Grouper? That's very peaceful after

lions. But I never shot an elephant.

They're too much like people. They live

in a family unit.

Victoria overhears the conversation and heard it all before.

Carl listens to Jimbo but watches Victoria as she goes out

on deck.

                            JIMBO

African pompano. I wont shoot just one

of them. They mate for life.

                            CARL

So, they're not like people.

EXT NIGHT YACHT

Victoria comes up behind Mitch who is massaging Annie's

shoulders.

                            VICTORIA

I'm not interrupting am I?

                            ANNIE

Oh, no.

                            MITCH

Join us. We'll do a menage a trois.

                            VICTORIA

I don't think Carl likes you.

                            MITCH

Let him take a number and stand in line.

                              ANNIE (to Victoria)

          When I was looking up at you're boat, I

          wanted so much to be here. And now that

          I'm here, I want to be back there.

Crew 3 comes by with a big lobster on a plate and takes it

inside to Carl.

                              ANNIE

          How do you live with it? With all of it!

                              VICTORIA

          Sometimes, too much of a good thing is

          not enough.

Mitch resumes rubbing Annie's neck.

                              MITCH

          That's what junkies say before they

          overdose.

                              VICTORIA (bothered)

          We all have our addictions. Mine is

          wealth. Yours is.... risk. Didn't you

          say, " No risk, no fun?"

Victoria moves closer until her body is touching Mitch's

arm. Crew 2 enters and they all turn to him. He is carrying

the soaking wet cat.

                              MITCH

          The rock must have come loose.It told

          Jimbo to do it right this time. Fleas,

          you know.

                        VICTORIA (irate)

You heartless son of a bitch.

                        ANNIE (to Victoria)

He's kidding. The cat swims.

                        VICTORIA (angry)

Don't defend him. I'm not stupid. I've

owned cats and they hate getting wet. I

can tolerate a lot in a man, but not

cruelty.

                        ANNIE (smells something)

It's the smell of the lobster.

                        VICTORIA (ignores Annie)

You think you can get away with this? I

can have you run out of here. Do you

know who I am.

                        MITCH (defiant)

Yeah, but who are you to me?

Victoria slaps Mitch across the face and he turns the other cheek.

INT NIGHT YACHT

Carl watches the scene outside from the table where he is

eating his lobster. He holds Jimbo back with his hand.

EXT NIGHT YACHT

Crew 2 hands the cat to Victoria and goes after Mitch who

has stepped away from Annie. As Crew 2 lunges, Mitch deftly

tosses him over the rail into the sea.

                        ANNIE (to Mitch)

Let's get Jimbo and our things and get

out of here.

                              VICTORIA (to Mitch)

          You're a pretty rough customer.

                              MITCH (smiles)

          Some people like it rough.

Victoria looks back over at the glass enclosed salon as she

strokes the cat.

                              VICTORIA

          And some people like it risky.

                              MITCH

          " No risk, no fun."

Holding the cat in one arm , Victoria reaches the other

around Mitches neck, pulls him to her and kisses him

fiercely. Annie looks back at the salon window.

POV ANNIE

INT NIGHT YACHT

Behind the glass Carl stands next to Jimbo glaring at the

scene.

EXT NIGHT YACHT

                              VICTORIA (bitter)

          Are we having fun yet.

Victoria turns their attention to the salon and walks away

stroking the cat.

EXT NIGHT DINGHY

Jimbo rows as Annie touches Mitch's mouth where he was

slapped.

                              ANNIE (worried)

          I think it's time to find another place

          to dive.

                              JIMBO (derisive)

          You're afraid of them.

                              MITCH (supportive)

          It is her charter.

                              JIMBO

          What about the dope?

                              MITCH

          We'll get some in the morning to take

          back and sell. The rest stays stashed

          for the future.

                              ANNIE

          What about Pus n' Boots.

                              MITCH

          He's only a cat.

INT NIGHT YACHT

The cat feeds on the lobster at the table. Victoria sits at
her desk while Carl pours another drink at the bar.

                              CARL

          You did it on purpose to make me

          jealous.

                              VICTORIA

          You go after game the way you want. I

          go after different game, it takes

          different methods.

Carl comes over behind Victoria. He grabs her neck in his
hands.

                         CARL

        You're mine. Do you understand?

                       VICTORIA

        No. You're mine. I can push one button

        on this machine and everything that the

        Senate wanted to know but was too stupid

        to ask will be public knowledge.

Victoria pulls away and goes over to the cat and strokes it.

                         CARL

        You're too much woman for me.

                       VICTORIA

        And if you ever grab me like that

        again, I'll scratch your eyes out.

        Now, run along. Don't you have something

        big to bag?

Carl turns to go and mutters under his breath.

                         CARL

        No bigger than a man.

EXT NIGHT BAY

The yacht and the trimaran sit quietly under the moon and

stars.

EXT NIGHT BOAT

Mitch sits alone on the bow staring at the yacht. Annie

comes up from the cabin wearing an oversized shirt that

comes just below her hips. She walks up to Mitch and stands

next to him. He doesn't look up.

                        ANNIE

        I feel like we're being thrown out of

        paradise.

                          MITCH

          You've got all the oceans to chose from.

                          ANNIE

          But I want to be here.

Mitch puts his hand down and pats Annie's foot while still
looking ahead.

                          MITCH

          It's your charter.

Mitch rests his hand on her instep. She doesn't pull away.

                          ANNIE

          I don't know.

Mitch begins to slowly massage the back of her calf.

                          MITCH

              Being on the outside wanting in, can be

              as bad as being on the inside wanting

              out. It depends on what you want.

                          ANNIE

              And what if you don't know what you

              want?

Mitch moves his hand up to massage her thigh.

                          MITCH

              Then you just take what's put before

              you.

Annie steps around so that she is standing over Mitch with
one foot to each side.

                          ANNIE

              I've learned one thing tonight.If you do

              see something you want, take it.

Annie kneels down and settles herself in Mitch's lap facing
him. She puts an arm around his neck, pulls him toward her
and kisses him. Then she looks at him. She speaks directly
as Victoria had done.

                        ANNIE

            Are we having fun yet?

They both laugh at her imitation.

                        MITCH

            Watch out, lady. I'm poison.

                        ANNIE

            That's what makes it fun.

She kisses him again and he embraces her pulling up her
shirt. She has nothing on underneath. Her tan line is clear.

                        MITCH

            Let's go down to my bunk.

                        ANNIE

            Damn, it's my period.

                        MITCH

            I've never been bothered by the sight of
            blood.

                        ANNIE

            Have you got condoms.

Mitch pulls a condom from his pocket. Annie blushes and
laughs.

                        ANNIE

            I'll bet you were a boy scout.

                        MITCH.

            No. A fortune teller.

INFARED SCOPE

EXT NIGHT BOAT

In the circular picture of black and red in the crosshairs of

an infared gunsight, Annie and Mitch are seen embracing. The

bathing suit shadow across Annie's rear end shows up bright

pink as she lifts her shirt over her head.

EXT NIGHT YACHT

Carl is looking through the scope on an automatic rifle as

he stands next to Crew 1 on the bridge of the yacht. Crew 1

is leaning against a search light dozing. He jumps alert

when Carl speaks.

                         CARL

              I told you if we waited long enough, we

              get our prey. I've got that diver and

              that rude girl together. We can kill two

              birds with one stone.

INFARED SCOPE

EXT NIGHT BOAT

In red and black and pink, we see Annie and Mitch in the

throes of passion. The crosshairs steady on the pink shadow.

                         CARL (OFF CAMERA)

              Steady. Steady. Squeeze. NOW!

There is the SOUND of a click and the scope flashes to

white.

EXT NIGHT BOAT

Annie and Mitch are caught full in the light of the

searchlight.

                              MITCH (yells)

            Son of a bitch!

EXT NIGHT BAY

The sharp white beam of the searchlight on the yacht

connects it to the trimaran. The SOUND of Carl & Crew

laughing goes across the water.

EXT NIGHT BOAT

Jimbo comes up from the cabin. He sees Annie naked on the

bow and Mitch pulling up his fly in the searchlight beam.

                              JIMBO

            What the hell is going on?

Annie pulls her shirt on. She tries to hide but Mitch holds

her in the spotlight.

                              MITCH

            Jimbo, have you got your slingshot?

Jimbo goes quickly below.

                              ANNIE (pleads)

            Let me go.

                              MITCH

            Hold still just for a minute.

Jimbo comes back on deck with the slingshot. He stays out of

the light and moves forward. He aims and the shot flies.

There is the SOUND of a crash and the light goes out. Jimbo

comes over to Mitch. He puts his hand out and Mitch slaps

it. Jimbo gives Annie a dirty look) Annie retreats to the cockpit.

                              JIMBO (to Mitch)

            What's going on.

                         MITCH (to Jimbo)

Remember. (instructionally) Jimbo,

pussy has nothing to do with the price

of pork. Do you understand?

                         JIMBO (nods)

Yeah, I get it.

Mitch puts out his hand and Jimbo slaps it. They both laugh.

Annie watches them from the cockpit. She breaths a sigh of

relief. She suddenly points to the yacht and yells.

                         ANNIE

Look out!

They all look at the sky.

EXT NIGHT BAY

An orange flare arcs across the darkness from the yacht and

splashes hissing into the water in front of the trimaran.

EXT NIGHT BOAT

Mitch looks at Jimbo and smiles. Annie stands holding her

shirt closed in front of her in the cockpit.

                         MITCH

        Two can play this game. Jimbo, get the

        gun.

Jimbo brushes past Annie going below.

                         ANNIE

No. Don't do this.

                         JIMBO

You, shut up!

Annie goes to Mitch and grabs his attention.

                          ANNIE

          Stop this. Stop it , now. You

          don't have to carry on this stupid

          fight. To prove what? For what?

                          MITCH

          It's just something men do.

                          ANNIE

          In that case I don't want any part

          of it.

                          MITCH

          You're on my boat. You are part of it.

          Are you with us or against us?

                          ANNIE

          Part of the solution or part of the

          problem?

                          MITCH

          Life is simple. I'm not the kind of man

          who runs from a fight.

                          ANNIE

          And what about the people who don't

          take sides.

                          MITCH

          They become refugees. (points to water)

          Go ahead, jump.

Annie goes down below passing Jimbo coming up with the flare

gun. Jimbo ignores her.

                          JIMBO

          I'll bet I can put one right down the

          stack.

                         MITCH
            Let's put on a little inspirational

            music.

EXT NIGHT BAY

A flare arcs from the trimaran to the yacht. The SOUND of

"The Star Spangled Banner " is heard in the background. Two

flares from the yacht fly at the trimaran. It answers back

with two of its own.

INT NIGHT BOAT

Annie is in her bunk looking at the ceiling. She looks

around but there is no place to go. She sees her camera

bag at her feet. She takes the camera bag to the

companionway and tosses it out. The SOUND of a splash is

heard. Annie turns and still there is no place to go.

She goes back to her bunk and stares at the cieling.

EXT NIGHT BAY

The rockets red glare and burst in the air.

EXT NIGHT BOAT

Mitch has the flare gun aimed at the yacht. A flare lands

on the deck and starts to burn. Jimbo kicks it overboard

and injures his foot.

                         MITCH (calls out)
            Annie, get up here fast and bring a

            bandage.

Annie sticks her head up and sees Jimbo lying on the deck

in pain. She comes up with a towel and disinfectant.

                         ANNIE (to Mitch)
            What am I now, a prisner of war?

Mitch fires at the yacht.

EXT NIGHT YACHT

Carl is at the rail directing his men. Crew 1 has a fire
extinguisher and is putting out a fire on deck. Crew 2 mans
the flare gun . Crew 3 stands by. Victoria storms out on
deck.

                         VICTORIA

          What in the hell do you juvenile

          delinquents think you're doing.?

                         CARL

          It's only a flare gun fight. Go back to

          bed.

                         VICTORIA

          Well an airliner saw your flares and

          reported it to the Coast Guard. They

          were starting a search and rescue

          operation when the radio operator woke

          me. I told them it was just a party

          that got out of hand. Now , stop it.

A flare bangs against the hull and fizzles in the water.
Carl picks up his automatic rifle.

                         CARL

          Okay, stop the music.I'll end it right

          now.

Carl shoves a clip into the rifle.

EXT NIGHT BOAT

Annie finishes wrapping Jimbo's foot. Mitch comes back to
the cockpit.

                         JIMBO

          I'm all right. But it hurts.

                         MITCH

          We're out of flares. I'll get the

          shotgun.

Annie goes to grab him as he turns toward the cabin.

Suddenly the SOUND of an automatic rifle clatters and

a row of small explosions smash along the outer hull.

Everyone stops in their tracks and loks at the damage.

                         ANNIE

          Now, I guess we know who has the

          biggest cock.

EXT NIGHT BAY

The trimaran and the yacht ride quietly at anchor under the

moon and the stars.

DISSOLVE TO

INT DAY BOAT

Mitch and Jimbo talk softly in the vee berth while Annie

sleeps in her bunk. Mitch takes a can from down below and

opens it for Jimbo. It has a ball of grey plastic and a

clock with wires.

                         MITCH

          Do you think you can swim with that

          foot?

                         JIMBO

          Easier than I can row. Where'd you get

          the plastic explosives?

                              MITCH

            It was left over from that demo job on

            St. Agnes. It's easy to use.

                              JIMBO

            I know how. I'm a diver too.

                              MITCH

            Then get a watch. I want this done

            right.

Jimbo goes into the main cabin to Annie's bunk. She is

sleeping with her back to him. On the shelf above her head

is the large silver dive watch from the airport. Jim

gingerly picks it up. Underneath it is the Freeze Frame

photo of Jimbo with the big lobster. Jimbo hobbles back

to Mitch.

                              JIMBO

            I've got it.

                              MITCH

            Okay, here's the plan. I go ashore and

            get the dope from the cave. You plant

            the plastique. Put it on one of the

            shafts outside the stuffing box. Give

            us pleanty of time to get out of here.

They go past Annie to get on deck. Annie turns over behind

them to watch them go.

EXT DAY YACHT

Victoria stands stroking the cat. Carl is standing next to

her with a pair of binoculars.

                         VICTORIA

          It's over. You've won.

                           CARL

          I don't want to just win. I want to beat

          him.

                         VICTORIA

          I'll put my money on the diver.

                           CARL

          In a fair fight, so would I.

                         VICTORIA

             Wait.

Carl leans over to kiss Victoria goodbye.. The cat swipes at

him and scratches his face. Carl goes to hit the cat. The

cat jumps from Victoria's arms runs along the deck down the

gangplank and jumps into the water.

                           CARL

             Well, isn't that the damndest thing!

             Gotta fly.

Victoria stands open mouthed watching the cat swim away as

Carl goes up to the helicopter pad.

EXT DAY BAY

Mitch rows away from the trimaran as the helicopter leaves

the yacht.

EXT DAY BOAT

Jimbo is on the net with his gear and one flipper when Annie

comes to him.

                          ANNIE

          Don't do it. Please, don't do it.

                         JIMBO

I'm just going for a little swim.

                         ANNIE

I know about the bomb. Somebody could

get killed.

                         JIMBO

Nobody will get killed. We're just going

to disable her.

                         ANNIE

That's what the French said when they

blew the Rainbow Warrior in New

Zealand.

                         JIMBO

I'm just going to blow the shaft.

                         ANNIE

What about the reef? What about the

fish? You love this place. You always

taught me to protect life underwater.

Only kill what you eat. Only take what

you need. Are we all hypocrites?Protect

what you love, Jimbo. You taught me

that.

                         JIMBO

It was just a line I stole from Jacques

Cousteau. This is different. It's a

matter of pride. Women don't understand.

Jimbo moves off the net into the water. Annie watches him

go. She is helpless. She is spent.

EXT DAY HELICOPTER

Carl pilots while 3 Crew crowd in with him.

                         CARL

              I'll set you down on the far side of the

              island. Work your way to the beach where

              his dinghy is . He's down there

              somewhere.

EXT DAY CAVE

Mitch surfaces in the pool inside the cave. He finds the

bale wrapped in a tarpaulin stashed between the rocks. He

cuts off three large chunks and puts them in three separate

plastic baggies.

EXT DAY BOAT

Annie sits waiting in the cockpit watching the shore. The

cat climbs up the towel and onto the boat. Annie tries to

smile but it only brings tears to her eyes.

EXT DAY YACHT

Victoria goes down the gangplank to the tender tied below.

She starts the engine and pulls away.

EXT DAY UNDERWATER

Jimbo dives down to the bottom and holds himself down by an

old rope on an old anchor. The SOUND of the tender pulling

away from the yacht fades. Jimbo watches it move off on the

surface above him. He notices the baracuda watching him.

Jimbo swims under the yacht. He sees the seafans waving

below him. He moves his hand to scatter a school of neon

striped fish surrounding the yacht's propeller shaft.

EXT DAY BAY

Victoria pilots the tender from the yacht to the trimaran.

Overhead, the helicopter buzzes angrily over the island.

INT DAY HELICOPTER

Carl is alone at the controls. He has a radio microphone

in one hand.

POV CARL

EXT DAY BEACH

Mitch is seen coming up out of the water by the beach near

his dinghy. The copter moves out to where the tender is

approaching the trimaran.

INT DAY HELICOPTER

Carl looks down.

                         CARL

            Too little to late. (in mike) Get to

            the beach fast. He was in the water.

EXT DAY BOAT

Victoria pulls up alongside the trimaran in the tender.

Annie gets up to meet her. She holds the cat.

                         VICTORIA

            Do you know where Mitch is?

                         ANNIE

            What do you want? You already gave him

            the kiss of death.

                         VICTORIA

            There's no time. Carl has taken three

            men to beat him.

Annie puts down the cat and gets in the tender.

EXT DAY BEACH

Mitch throws the three baggies into the dinghy and starts

to push off when Crew 2 and Crew 3 come up behind him. One

man has a club and the other has a knife. Without hesitation

Mitch takes one of the oars from his dinghy and smashes it

against the head of Crew 3 with the knife. Mitch puts so

much force and viciousness into the blow that it shatters

the oar with the SOUND of a tremendous clout. The man with

the club steps back when he sees he companion crumble to the

ground.

EXT DAY BAY

The tender rushes through the water and plows up on the

shore.

EXT DAY BEACH

Mitch is distracted by the incoming dinghy with Annie and

Victoria jumping out. Crew 3 with the club lunges at Mitch

catching him in the ribs with the club. Annie screams.

Crew 3 turns toward Annie as she rushes at him. He is taken

by surprise as she keeps coming at him. Annie sticks her

fingers in his eyes. He drops the club and staggers holding

his face. Annie takes the heel of her hand and strikes him

under in the nose causing a torrent of blood. Victoria is

at Mitch's side. He is in pain but functional.

                              VICTORIA

                    That's only two of them.

Crew 1 comes out of the jungle. He has a gun pointed at

Mitch. Victoria steps between Mitch and the gun. Mitch

tries to push her aside but can't because of the pain in

his ribs.

                         VICTORIA

          This is all my fault. (to Crew 1) Put

          away the gun. (shouts) I'm the one

     .   that pays you. Now, give me that gun.

Crew 1 puts away the gun and goes to help his fallen

comrades. Mitch and Annie get into the dinghy.

                         MITCH (to Victoria)

          Come with us.

                         VICTORIA ·

          I can't leave them. They're my

          responsibility. I'll see you back home.

                    .   MITCH

          Give us a head start.

Victoria helps push the dinghy out and starts Annie starts

paddling. Mitch holds his ribs.

EXT DAY BAY

As the dinghy pulls away from the beach with Annie paddling

with one oar and Mitch reclining in the bow, the helicopte

hovers above the beach.

EXT DAY BOAT

Jimbo is waiting on the trimaran. He helps Mitch get on

board as Annie ties off the dinghy. Jimbo sees bloodon the

front of Annie's clothes.

                         JIMBO

          What happened to you?

                         ANNIE

          It's that time of month. Let's get out

          of here.

DISSOLVE TO

EXT DAY BAY

The trimaran sails out past the yacht; Annie at the wheel and

Jimbo hobbles back from the mast to the cockpit where

Mitch is wrapping his ribs. The helicopter passes low

overhead.

EXT DAY BOAT

The trimaran moves along under sail. Mitch grabs Jimbo's

hand and looks at his watch.

                              JIMBO

          We have plenty of time.

                              MITCH

          Did you set it like I told you?

Jimbo looks at Annie. Annie looks at the two of them and

frowns.

                              ANNIE

          Shit. Damn it. Son of a bitch.

                              JIMBO (to Mitch)

          She knows. She overheard the plan.

                              ANNIE

          I'm such an airhead!

                              MITCH

          You're anything but an airhead.

                              ANNIE

          I was so worried about saving your

          rotten neck that I forgot to tell

          Victoria about the bomb.

Jimbo picks up one of the plastic bags with the big chunk of
marijuana in it.

> JIMBO
>
> Don't worry she won't get hurt. (hefts
> bag) At least it wasn't a wasted trip.
> That's about a pound for each of us.

> ANNIE
>
> You can have mine. When we get back, I'm
> going home.

DISSOLVE TO

EXT DAY OCEAN

The trimaran under full sail moves with the wind. The island
is in the background. Jimbo is at the wheel. Mitch is
stretched out on the cockpit cushion.

EXT DAY BOAT

Annie comes up from down below. Jimbo stands at the wheel,
his knee resting on a water drum to ease his injured foot.
Mitch gets up from his cushion in much pain. He looks at
Jimbo's watch. Jimbo pulls his hand away. He takes off the
watch and offers it to Annie.

> JIMBO
>
> This belongs to you.

> ANNIE
>
> No thanks. Give it to your girlfriend.

> MITCH
>
> It should be soon. (looks back toward
> island) We should be able to hear it.

                          ANNIE

Will that make your ribs feel better?

                          MITCH

Yeah, it sure will. That lady will

survive. You didn't have to tell her.

                          ANNIE

You didn't tell her either.

                          MITCH

Never tell them everything.

                          ANNIE (explodes)

Fuck you. I'm tired of all your he man

bullshit. The woman saved your fucking

life and you didn't have the common

decency to return the favor.

                          JIMBO

Calm down , Annie.

                          ANNIE

Fuck you too.

                          MITCH (yells)

Everybody shut the fuck up. I want to

hear it blow.

Mitch painfully stands up and turns back toward the island.

                          JIMBO

You won't be able to hear it.

                          MITCH

We're not that far away. If you set it

right, we'll hear it.

                         JIMBO

There won't be any explosion.

                         ANNIE

What do you mean?

                         MITCH

You said you knew how to use that stuff.

                         JIMBO

I didn't plant the bomb.

                         MITCH (incredulous)

You didn't? That was the plan. (his

anger builds) You were supposed to blow

it. That was the fucking plan, man. Do

you know what happens in a war when you

don't stick to the plan. Somebody dies.

Mitch moves in on Jimbo and raises his fist. Jimbo lets go

of the wheel and turns on Mitch. Annie steps in between

them.

                         ANNIE (yells)

Mitch. The war is over. This isn't the

Navy. The war is over. No one is going

to die.

Mitch catches his breath and calms down. He moves in at the

wheel and takes over for Jimbo even though he is in pain.

                         MITCH

They'll catch us. They'll catch us and

they've got more fire power than we do.

Jimbo, get the shotgun.

                            JIMBO

          They won't catch us. I tied the shaft to

          an old anchor rode on the bottom. They'll

          fouled for hours, maybe days.

Mitch is silent as he steers the boat. Annie and Jimbo sit

down and she fixes the bandage on his foot.

                            ANNIE (softly)

          What made you change your mind?

                            JIMBO (embarrassed)

          A baracuda.

                            ANNIE

          Our baracuda?

                            JIMBO

          Our baracuda.

Mitch ignores them, steering in obvious pain and muttering

to himself.

                            MITCH

          The plan. He should have stuck to the

          plan.

EXT DAY HELICOPTER

Carl pilots the helicopter while Victoria sits next to him.

Carl points below.

                            CARL

          There they are.

                            VICTORIA

          It's over. Let them alone.

                            CARL

          It's over when I say it's over.

POV CARL

EXT DAY OCEAN

The helicopter dives down toward the top of the trimaran's

mast.

REVERSE ANGLE

EXT DAY BOAT

The helicopter buzzes the mast top.   Annie, Jimbo and

Mitch instinctively duck as the helicopter flies by.

Victoria can be seen giving a thumbs up sign in the window

of the helicopter as it flies away.

                              MITCH

                    There's something I like about that

                    dame. Something special. But, he bother

                    me a lot. Jimbo, come on take over at

                    ·the wheel. I have to lay down.

Jimbo takes the helm. Annie helps Mitch to the cockpit

cushion.

                              JIMBO

                    You're not worried about a guy like that

                    are you?

                              MITCH

                    A guy like that can pay a guy like me to

                    take care of a guy like me.

                              ANNIE

                    Don't worry about it. Just rest.

Annie sits on the floor of the cockpit near Mitch.

                        MITCH

I never thought I'd take orders

from a woman.

                        ANNIE

Is that so bad?

                        MITCH

When you're a kid, you look around at

the characters in your life and you

decide which one you want to be and

that's the kind of person you grow into.

Doctor. Pirate. Hero. Villain. You just

never think of that character growing

old.

                        ANNIE

You're not old.

                        MITCH

I'm not young. There was a time when it

would have taken more than a couple of

broken ribs to stop me. Did I ever thank

you?

Mitch sticks out his hand and Annie holds it in her hand.

Mitch closes his eyes.

EXT DAY ANCHORAGE

The trimaran is at anchor in the harbor. Nearby a trawler

rides at anchor. The SOUND of a pump can be heard as the

trawler pumps its bilges. A small powerboat with a Coast

Guard insignia approaches the trimaran. An OFFICER, a

CREWMAN and a DOG are in the boat.

EXT DAY BOAT

Annie sits on the side of the cockpit with the cat in her

lap. Jimbo has a sail draped over his injured foot and works

on a patch with a needle and yarn. Mitch comes up slowly

from the cabin as the Coast Guard boat with the two men and

the dog pull up astern. He has a pot of coffee in his hand.

                    OFFICER

          Permission to come aboard.

                    MITCH

          Permission granted.

The Crewman ties off on a stern cleat and he and the Officer

and the dog come on board in their neat white uniforms.

                    MITCH

          What can we do for you? We were just

          having coffee.

                    OFFICER

          No, thank you. And keep it away from

          the dog. It throws his nose off. Do

          you mind if we look around?

                    MITCH

          What are you looking for?

                    OFFICER

          We think that trawler over there dumped

          a load of contraband offshore. It's been

          washing up on the reef. It's Panamanian

          registered. We're waiting for orders to

          sieze it.

                        JIMBO

     By the time you get your orders, he'll

     have pumped out everything but the

     bottom paint.

The officer scows at Jimbo. He motions to the Crewman

holding the dog.

                        OFFICER

     Let's take a look below.

The Officer starts down the companionway. Mitch is close

behind him. The Crewman and the dog squeeze between Jimboand

his sail and Annie with the cat. The dog growls at the cat.

Jimbo tries to move the sail out of the way.

                        JIMBO (to Crewman)

     Watch your step.

The Crewman looks down. Jimbo pulls up on the sail knocking

him off balance.

                        CREWMAN

     Ohh, shit.

Annie reaches out to steady him and drops the cat on the

dog. The Officer steps up from the cabin to see what is

going on . He bumps into Mitch who spills coffee on his

white uniform, stumbles backward and spills coffee on the

Crewman and the dog. The cat runs away from the dog and

jumps in the water. The dog gives chase, tries to stop at

the transom and tumbles overboard.

                        OFFICER (to Crewman)

     Look what you've done now, you clumsy

     son of a bitch. Coffee leaves stains.

EXT DAY ANCHORAGE

The Coast Guard boat pulls away from the trimaran with the
wet dog in the stern barking at the cat in the water.

INT NIGHT BOAT

Mitch is layed out in his bunk with the cat on his chest. He
smiles and holds his ribs. Annie and Jimbo are in their
bunks laughing out loud.

                    JIMBO

          Did you see the look on his face when
          Mitch spilled the coffee on his whites?

                    ANNIE

          It worked perfectly.

                    MITCH

          That was the plan.

                    JIMBO

          We make a good team.

                    ANNIE

          Good old Pus. He's some cat.

                    JIMBO

          Mitch, what's the plan for tomorrow?

                    MITCH

          I'll go in and see about selling the
          dope. You go to the airport and change
          Annie's ticket and we meet back at the
          Non-Select.

                    ANNIE

          And I'll stay here and pack.

                         MITCH

         I wish you'd change your mind. You make

         great crew.

                         ANNIE

         There must be more to life.

Annie looks at the ceiling of her bunk.

EXT DAY ANCHORAGE

The dinghy pulls away from the trimaran with Mitch and

Jimbo. In the distance the yacht can be seen at the quay.

DISSOLVE TO

INT DAY BAR

Jimbo sits at the bar with a beer and an airline ticket in

front of him. He looks at his watch. Dee is in front of him.

She has a red flower in her hair.

                         DEE

         For days. Everybody been selling. One

         hundred dollars a pound. Fifty dollars

         a pound. They be getting off the reef.

         Twentyfive dollars a pound, wet.

Jimbo touches the flower in her hair. He is preoccupied.

Mitch comes in from the street entrance and sits down next

to Jimbo. Dee gets him his lime water. Mitch sets a nylon

bag on the counter.

                         JIMBO (to Mitch)

         Looks full. Bad day for the dog, mon?

                         MITCH

         You can't give it away.

                              JIMBO

          I saw the helicopter at the airport. I

          checked it out. He filed a flight plan

     .   to leave today.

Jimbo looks at his watch.

                              MITCH (irritated)

          I told you not to wear that around here.

          Have you seen anybody get off the boat?

Dee has been listening and takes a piece of paper from under

the bar.

                              DEE

          I almost forgot. This come from the lady

          on the big boat.

Mitch takes the note and reads it. A big smile comes to his

lips.

                              MITCH

          The lady writes that her husband is

          leaving today. She wants to meet me at

          her cabana at the casino.

                              JIMBO

          Are you sure it's safe.

                              MITCH

          I trust this lady.

                              JIMBO

          Do you want me to take care of the bag?

                              MITCH

          No, I'll take it with me. She might want

          to party hard.

                        JIMBO

        There's something special about older

        women that you like isn't there?

                        MITCH

        Yeah, they don't pee on the rug.

Mitch leaves some money onthe bar.

                        JIMBO

        So, what's the plan?

                        MITCH

        After you take Annie to the airport,

        I'll meet you back here.

Mitch goes out by the street entrance. Jimbo starts playing

with the coins amusing Dee.

                        DEE

        That's a mighty pretty watch.

                        JIMBO

        You like?

                        DEE

        I like.

Jimbo takes her hand in his . He holds her wrist. When he

opens his hand, she wears the watch. Jimbo suddenly turns

serious.

                        JIMBO

        Did the lady drop off that message.

                        DEE

        No, it was one of the mens.

Jimbo rushes out the street entrance.

EXT DAY CABANA

Mitch walks along a path to the door of a cabana set back

among the coconut palms. Mitch straightens his cap with the

dive insignia and knocks on the door. The door opens. The

SOUND of a gunshot echoes in the blackness.

EXT DAY CASINO

Jimbo tries to get through a small crowd that has formed in

front of an elegant building. The Island Cop is holding

people back.

                         JIMBO

          What happened?

                         COP

          Drug deal gone bad, mon. Found three

          bags still on him. You know the mon.

TWO ATTENDANTS in white uniforms roll out a stretcher with

a body on it covered with a blood stained sheet. Jimbo

breaks through the crowd and pulls the sheet off. Mitch

is dead on the stretcher.

                         COP

          Get back, mon. Hey, what be doing? Wait.

          Wait!

Jimbo runs away.

INT DAY BOAT

Annie has her bags ready on her bunk. The cat is next to

them. There is the SOUND of footsteps on deck. Jimbo comes

down into the cabin. He throws the airline ticket at Annie

and searches in his bunk.

                          ANNIE

What's wrong? Where's Mitch?

                     JIMBO (angry)

Mitch is dead.

                     ANNIE (gasps)

It can't be.

Jimbo takes the plastic explosive and the timer from his

bunk and puts it in his backpack.

                          JIMBO

I should have stuck to the plan. That

son of a bitch set a trap for Mitch and

he fell for it. Because of a woman.

                          ANNIE

What are you going to do?

                          JIMBO

I'm going to get even.

                          ANNIE

He died the way he lived. The law of the

jungle. You said it yourself. Big fish

eat little fish.

                          JIMBO

And some little fish are poison. ⋅ Come

on, I'll take you to the airport.

                          ANNIE

Jimbo....

                          JIMBO

Shut up, and get in the dinghy.

INT DAY YACHT

Victoria enters the salon of the yacht. She goes over to her

desk. She suddenly looks up as something on the trophy wall

gets her attention. She walks over to the Ram's head.

Hanging on one of the horns is Mitch's cap with the

insignia.

EXT DAY BOAT

The cat sits on the back of the boat all alone and watches

the dinghy pull away with Annie and Jimbo.

INT DAY AIRPORT

Annie stands in line at the check in counter. Behind her the

window of the gift shop is boarded up. The Island Cop can be

seen in the doorway talking to Dee. Annie is oblivious to

everything. Jimbo comes up behind Annie.

                         JIMBO

             It's all taken care of.

                         ANNIE

             I don't want to hear about it.

                         JIMBO

             About the stash. I'll send you back your

             travelers checks after I go back to the

             boat. The charter was for free.

                         ANNIE (holds back tears)

             Do you think I care about money now?

                         JIMBO

             I'm sorry I....

                          ANNIE

          Don't apologize someone might think you

          mean it.

The Island Cop holding Dee by the arm comes over to Jimbo.

Dee points at Jimbo. Annie steps back.

                           DEE

          That's him. Him gave me the watch.

                           COP

          You are under arrest, mon.

                          JIMBO

          I didn't do anything wrong!

EXT DAY AIRPORT

Jimbo is in the back seat of an Island police car. Annie is

at the window talking to him.

                          JIMBO (protests)

          I'm innocent.

The SOUND of a helicopter is heard overhead. Jimbo and Annie

look up.

POV ANNIE

EXT DAY SKY

The helicopter gets higher and higher in the sky as it flies

out over the water. The helicopter explodes.

EXT DAY AIRPORT

The SOUND of the explosion thunders down to Annie and Jimbo.

Jimbo sits back in the seat. There is a lot of confusion as

people come out of the terminal to see what happened. The

police car with Jimbo inside starts to pull away.

                          ANNIE

         Jimbo, what can I do.

Jimbo sticks his head out the window.

                          JIMBO

         Don't forget to feed the cat.

The car pulls away leaving Annie at the entrance of the

terminal amid the confusion.

DISSOLVE TO

EXT NIGHT BOAT

The colors of the sunset fill the sky. Annie sits in the

cockpit stroking the cat. The SOUND of a motor boat gets

louder and stops. Annie looks back over the transom. She

sees Mitch's cap with the insignia.

                          ANNIE? (startled)

         Mitch!

Victoria's head comes up under the cap as she secures the

tender to a stern cleat and climbs aboard. She comes over

to Annie. She takes off the cap and gives it to her.

                          VICTORIA

         I know what happened. They're both dead.

                          ANNIE

         Bad day for the dog, mon.

Annie stands up and the two women hold each other for a

moment. Then they sit down across from each other. The

cat goes over to Victoria and she pets it.

                          VICTORIA

         What are you going to do?

                         ANNIE

    I think maybe I'll go back to Money Bay

    and cry for a while and eat brownies.

                        VICTORIA

    Alone? Isn't that risky.

Annie puts the cap on her head and forces a smile.

                         ANNIE

    You know what the man said. " If you're

    not taking a risk, you're not having

    any fun." What about you?

                        VICTORIA

    Maybe I'll look for a fifth husband. Or

    maybe I'll   RETURN TO MONEY BAY *

                         ANNIE

    We can always use good crew.

The two women sit silently and watch the stars come out.

FADE OUT

                        THE END

    * The sequel